Tom Bullough

Sort Of Books

LONDON

For Fay

Thanks

TOM: Boundless thanks to C, J, **Matthew**, O and W (alph. order), Nat, Mark, the incredible Hughes and Llewellyn families, Michael Morrogh, Dave for acidic advice (*daveyx@hotmail.com*), Angus, Oshry, Carl, Bruce Robinson, Peter Dyer, Ian Lowe, Mary and Becky.

SORT OF thanks: Peter Dyer, Henry Iles, Nikky Twyman, Caroline Natzler, Giovanna Iannaco, and, at Penguin, Liz Statham, Lucy Green, Lance Chinnian and Mark Barrow.

Published in June 2002 by SORT OF BOOKS, PO Box 18678, London NW3 2FL
www.sortof.co.uk

Distributed by the Penguin Group in all territories excluding the United States and Canada by Penguin Books, 80 Strand, London WC2R 0RL

Typeset in Goudy to a design by Henry Iles
Printed in the UK by Clays, Bungay, Suffolk
240pp.

A catalogue record for this book is available from the British Library
ISBN 0-9535227-6-8

Acknowledgments

Tom Bullough and Sort Of Books gratefully acknowledge the following copyright permissions:

I'LL BE SEEING YOU Words by Irving Kahal © 1938 Williamson Music Inc – Redwood Music Ltd (Carlin), London NW1 8BD, for the Commonwealth of Nations, Eire, South Africa and Spain – All Rights Reserved – Used by Permission.

THE THRILL IS GONE by Lew Brown and Ray Henderson © 1931 De Sylva, Brown & Henderson Inc – Redwood Music Ltd (Carlin), London NW1 8BD, for the Commonwealth of Nations, Germany, Austria, Switzerland, South Africa and Spain – All Rights Reserved – Used by Permission.

STREET OF DREAMS Words and Music by Sam Lewis and Victor Young © 1932 EMI Catalogue Partnership, EMI Feist Catalog Inc and EMI United Partnership Ltd, USA. Worldwide print rights controlled by Warner Bros. Publications Inc/IMP Ltd. Reproduced by kind permission of International Music Publications Ltd – All Rights Reserved.

AMBULANCE BLUES by Neil Young © Neil Young – Wixen Music Publishing – Warner Bros Publications – All Rights Reserved – Used by Permission.

Sugasugashii
Refreshing

Bofuu no ato ni
After the gale

Tsuki kyo shi
The moon rises, shining

Admiral Takijiro Onishi, 15 August 1945
a haiku written for his suicide

a: voice of the crane

The music was funky, with a hip-hop beat and a vocoder over the top of it. The two vehicles were flying round the M25, the heat building banks of distortion behind and in front of them, blotting out everything beyond. With wooded verges to either side, their piece of space might almost have been all there was; except, of course, for the endless blue of the sky – a rare buzzard floating on the updraughts, twitching its wings with lazy, occasional movements.

Pete's ambulance had hung beside Tim's car for miles, or Tim's car had hung beside it. It was the nine of them being together at last – that and the sense of occasion – it seemed to require a gesture. So they occupied parallel lanes, and there was nothing anyone else could do about it.

Pete had his shirt off, the sun on his stomach. He had wrap-around sunglasses and his dreadlocks loose down his back, one hand on the steering-wheel, the other drumming on the panelling beneath the window. Fay and Katy were lounging beside him. Katy was laughing, moving her hands in sinuous patterns. Wedged against the window, Fay was sunning herself, catlike. From time to time Nick stuck his head in from the back, releasing bong-sized clouds of smoke or sticking up a finger in the others' direction. Sunlight traced the dents across the blank white Transit walls.

In the Nissan, a new tune was evolving on the stereo. This one was faster, a 303 mounting in the background. When the beat kicked in Paolo shouted from the back seat, gesturing for more volume, his bulbous Afro shaking on the offbeat. He had REGGAE in big square letters across his chest and a heap of seafood in Tupperware boxes on his lap: mussels and prawns, salmon, tuna and cuttlefish.

> Kingston said a sign and Tim led the way down the banked arc of a sliproad, leaning into the curve like a biker. He came vertical as the road went straight, eyes glued to the car in front, changing mechanically down through the gears.

Next to Paolo, a pair of bodies were untangling themselves.

– Hello, Belle whispered to Angus. She smiled, brushing a few strands of blonde hair out of her eyes.

– Hello, Angus whispered back.

Belle shuffled closer on the cracked brown seat-cover, putting an arm around his neck, closing her eyes, smiling again as he kissed her.

The house in Kingston was a great old wreck of a place: a 1950s dreamhouse, crumbling and swamped in creepers. It stood out against the rest of Burnell Road like a tramp at a convention of estate agents. Over the past twenty years or so the shrubberies bordering the pavement had turned into ashes, sycamores and rhododendrons so enormous they didn't seem entirely natural. They groped at the air above the yard, splattering shadows across chippings, weeds and wandering herbaceous borders.

The house itself was brilliant in the midday sunshine. At some point during the past week the hydrangea had come into flower. It smothered the wall in front of them with gleaming white petals, closing round the windows and clambering across the roof.

– Look! It's gift-wrapped! said Fay delightedly, jumping from the passenger door of the ambulance and sniffing at the heavy smell of blossom.

– It's ours! hissed Paolo. He poked Angus in the ribs, grinning idiotically. I mean, get in! It's fucking ours!

But there remained an air of solemnity as the others extracted themselves and converged around the front door. Paolo, Tim, Katy, Fay, Belle, Nick, Pete and Angus. They were in a tidy kind of semicircle when Rob produced the key from his pocket: tall, Indian, with little round sunglasses and floppy black hair. For a moment he let it hover, then he floated it towards the lock – slowly, like he was introducing food to a baby – and pushed wide the door.

– The HQ! he announced, stepping to one side.

Although they had all viewed the house, a week or so earlier, it seemed somehow changed as they looked across the dusty carpet – the sofa, the bookshelves, a table, a couple of old chairs – through the French windows and out across the overgrown lawn towards the listing iron fence, the towpath, the river twinkling in the background.

– Da paura! observed Paolo finally, breaking the stupefaction. Wicked! He strode into the living-room, a family of whole prawns peering from halfway up his chest. Then Belle and Katy rushed in after him, vanishing up the stairs; and the rest of them followed.

Inside the house was cool, musty from years of isolation. They spread themselves up stairs and around rooms, breathing like even the air was on the inventory. They found slides in the attic: the perfect 1950s couple posed before the wonders of the world. They found a collection of broken washing machines at the bottom of the back stairs; a set of *British Empire* magazines in gold-embossed maroon binders in one of the bedrooms; a barbecue set sitting ready on the patio.

Everywhere there were bursts of laughter, the sounds of people jumping down the stairs. To have found somewhere so cheap, and so large, was incredible enough, but the real

3

excitement was in escaping the university: the students' union, with its '70s nights and alcopop promotions, the halls of residence, their concrete corridors and endless daytime television. If there was one thing that had brought them all together, it was a loathing of the place. And now they were suddenly emancipated. The feeling was euphoric, almost as if they were floating.

The other thing, of course, being that they all took a lot of drugs. Not that there was anything very unusual about this, but it was how most of them had met up in the first place: looking for somewhere to score and picking out the most likely-looking people to ask.

– Radioactives, Tim was droning in his usual monotone, pointing out the symbols on the little white tablets to the two or three people watching. They're really great. Ninety-five percent MDMA and the other five caffeine. A friend of mine in the Chemistry department – you know, Dave? Three-eyed Dave? – he tested one so, like, it's official…

Tim was bending over a three-legged coffee table in the living-room – greasy-haired, in jeans and a sweatshirt – collecting the pills into piles. Rob rubbed his hands on his loose, stripy trousers.

4

– E-ecstasy! he shouted at the stairwell.

A kind of ripple passed outwards through the house. Someone stopped bouncing on a bed. Someone else whooped in the attic. The garden door clacked open. Then the banisters started rattling: Belle and Katy stampeded down the stairs. Paolo and Nick trotted in from the kitchen. The queue began coming together.

It was part of Tim's approach to these things that each person's chemicals be dispensed individually. This allowed him both to tick off who owed what in his notebook and to perform a sort of reverend role as the dispenser. He sat behind the coffee table, jotting down debits, credits and quantities, and occasionally looking up with an expression like a bank manager's.

– Ketamine? he asked Angus, as he handed him his pill. 2C-B? Acid?

Angus was looking healthy at this point in time: sun-browned, long-haired, with thin, defined arms and a sleeveless black T-shirt. Around him the living-room was crowded – people were milling about, accepting joints and washing down pills – and it took him a moment to locate Belle beside the window, talking to Rob, presumably about India. It was never a conversation he could add very much to. It seemed better to go and take the pill, and retrieve her when he was feeling a bit more empowered.

The kitchen had a chequered blue linoleum floor and a series of light-blue sideboards. Angus scraped his hair back from his face, pulling himself onto one of them and weighing the pill in his left hand as he ran the tap till it came through cold. He filled a glass and drank some water, but when it came to actually putting the pill in his mouth he found – inexplicably – that he couldn't.

His arms had become lifeless.

Above the house a plane was falling – howling – towards Heathrow. Sitting on the sideboard, Angus was starting to sweat; a droplet appeared on his palm, sucking off a corner of the pill. It was like having forgotten the name of someone incredibly famous: Elvis, for instance. Angus knew that he could operate his arms, but whenever he attempted to grasp the knowledge it just slipped further away.

Others had started to appear in the kitchen now, heading for the garden – Pete, Tim, Paolo – a pill or two under their

5

belts, laughing expectantly. They glanced at Angus as they passed, nodded; but it was only when Nick shuffled in a minute later that he found himself able to speak.

Nick stopped in the middle of the floor, his hands in his pockets, a sunburnt bald patch in the crown of his sandy hair.

– Not had your pills? he said.

– No... said Angus weakly.

– Why's that then? You've gone all white, do you know that?

– I don't know, said Angus. I don't fucking know! My arms are stuck!

– You look freaked, said Katy, arriving beside Nick. She gestured towards the garden. You should get outside, you know? Get some air in.

Angus dropped the dissolving pill on the sideboard, and followed her through the washing-room, past the bottom of the back stairs.

Out on the patio, Katy peeled off her shirt, tugging down her vest to conceal her fleshy waist. Paolo was already reclining in a deckchair he appeared to have found in the shrubbery. He had assumed a look of authority, one eye on Tim, to whom he'd delegated control of the barbecue.

– Alright, Ang? he said.

– Alright, said Angus weakly, looking round the garden for a place to collapse.

6   All he really wanted now was Belle, to come and put her arms round him and make him feel whole again. But she was still there in the living-room; he could see her through the French windows, listening to Rob.

The garden was long and thin, wildly overgrown, with the former hedges craning in from either side of it: hollies, beeches and flowering laburnums. Pete was spreadeagled on the grass about halfway to the river, far enough from the shadows not to have to move for some time. His eyes were closed behind his sunglasses, the sun on his stomach stared upwards, a ragged book of Japanese prints lay open beside him that Angus had found that week in a second-hand bookshop.

Angus sat unsteadily, pulling a packet of cigarettes from his combats and lighting one, picking up the book and flicking through a few pages.

– Give us one, said Pete, his eyes still closed. What are they, Marlboro?

– Lights, said Angus, dropping one into his hand.

– Cheers, said Pete.

For a moment he rolled it between his thumb and forefinger, then he opened his left eye and put it in his mouth, taking a Zippo from a pocket of his jeans and flicking the wheel till it caught.

– Wicked book, he said, coughing smoke and pulling himself upright. A bit kind of disciplined, but the colours are amazing... What's going on?

– Weird shit, said Angus. Some very weird shit. Pete. I... I couldn't take that pill.

– How do you mean?

– I tried to but I couldn't move my arms. I was just sitting on the sideboard, staring at the fucking thing, and I couldn't move them! It was like... like they were fucking paralysed or something!

Pete inspected him over his sunglasses, squint-eyed.

7

– But, they're okay now?

– Yeah. Angus sucked nervously on his cigarette.

– And you feel alright?

– No, I don't feel fucking alright!

– Okay, okay, said Pete. Look, let's get a handle on this, yeah? It's a new one on me. You wanted to take a pill, but you were not able to... Are you sure you actually wanted to take it?

– Of course I am, said Angus.

Pete put the cigarette in his mouth and tied his dreadlocks back.

– Why, then?

– Why?! Angus echoed. Well, why did you? Why would anyone? To enjoy myself. To make the most of the moment. To feel… alive!

He petered out.

A few yards away Belle and Rob had emerged on the patio. Belle had removed her shirt and was wearing a croptop, her chest at its most spectacular.

– You know, Rob was peering at her through his sunglasses. Altamont was really the Fall. Do you know what I mean? When the dream was revealed for itself? It was like, an epiphany of man's humanity; and woman's too, of course… He smiled inclusively. So, as I see it, our task with this group is to rebuild that dream, but to work from an enlightened standpoint. To re-attain Eden, if you like.

– Wow! said Belle, smiling enlightenedly.

She was obviously coming up, starting to chew.

– What did you say again? said Pete, following Angus's eyes.

– So, Belle, I suppose what I'm really asking you is: Are you ready to see God?

8

The sound of Rob's voice – his guru posturing – was making Angus's blood go strange. He knew perfectly well now why he'd wanted to take the pill: Belle. It was that simple. If the pills were even half as good as Tim had made out, she'd have been all over him, and he'd have been all over her, and it would have been just like it had been when they first got together – even if it was only for a few hours.

– Well? said Pete.

The clamour of a train was floating upstream from the

bridge. An eight was rowing hard by the end of the garden, the cox squealing instructions.

– Let's go down to the river, said Angus.

A couple of willows leant out across the water a little way upstream of the end of the garden, and just between them a small white cabin cruiser of a similar vintage to the house was moored against the bank. Pete and Angus sat down on the grass beside it, smoking fat roll-ups and watching a flotilla of swans slip round a bush, necks like unconvincing glove puppets. Pete was beginning to rock with pleasure.

– What do you get for eight magpies? asked Fay, appearing and sitting down beside them.

– What? said Angus.

– Well, there's eight magpies over there. She pointed at the lawn of the rowing club across the river: a cluster of magpies around something dead. It's seven for a story never to be told. What happens next?

Angus looked at her: thin, cheekbones, a pair of loose blue trousers. She was the only other person around not coming up on anything. If only for that it was nice to see her.

– A set of cut-glass tumblers? she suggested.

Angus chuckled.

– A Black & Decker workbench, he said. There's always a Black & Decker workbench.

For a second it was like a path had opened beside him – the dread evaporating – but even as he realised, it was already too late. The opening had passed, and he'd been no more able to turn towards it than he'd been to move his arms.

– How are the pills? said Fay.

– They set my soul on fire, Pete muttered, rocking back and forth, his eyes on the swans.

9

– Oh, no pills for me, said Angus. I mean... Look at this! He waved a hand at the river, trying to muster conviction. It's such a beautiful day. I didn't really see the need...

Fay narrowed her eyes. They were green already but greener in sunlight; they made Angus feel like she was seeing right through him. He held the look for three or four seconds, then he turned towards the swans.

Angus had only actually spoken to Fay a half-dozen times or so before but every occasion had been very much the same. She was Katy's best friend, a fellow Psychology student, and the obvious person to ask when the house proved larger than the group was. She fitted in well, considering – sharing the others' views on the university – but somehow she was on a different wavelength, a bit of a loner. You had to be to stay straight with everyone else in that condition.

Angus realised suddenly that the look had been one of concern.

– Hey! came a shout from behind them.

The rest of the household was nearing the end of the garden, grinning feverishly. Belle was at the front, her arms round Katy, giggling and talking, a bindi glittering on her forehead. Tim handed her an enormous menthol joint. Further back towards the patio, Angus noticed, Paolo was brushing dust from Nick's shoulder. They were talking intently, their heads held closely together, pointing up at the roof of the house.

– Hiya! said Belle, squeezing through the gate. She bent down and put an arm round Angus's neck, kissing him, pushing her tongue between his lips.

– Hi, he said afterwards, swamped equally in panic and desire.

Belle was flushed, her jaw working excitedly. She grinned and pressed herself against him – lustful – her nipples hard through the thin cloth. It was how she got on a decent pill: just like Angus had predicted.

– I'm in heaven! she told him ardently. How about you?

– I… For a few seconds Angus said nothing, reluctant to lie about it. Well. Belle, I didn't actually take anything.

Belle's chewing stopped.

– What…? she said. Her forehead creased. Her voice was almost mournful. No! Angus, you're not serious?!

Bit by bit, Belle slipped away from him, to Katy and Rob and the others. Angus knew it was happening but he might have been stone; there wasn't a thing he could do about it.

It was a bit like a cartoon, where a scheming-eyed cat in a boiler suit switches the railway points; so the train containing the treasure of the Sierra Madre heads straight on east across the desert, while the train in pursuit gets sucked away onto another track, steaming in parallel with the first perhaps for a minute or two before turning in a great, inevitable arc among the cacti and vanishing back west.

The future was laid out like that, Angus realised: nailed to sleepers, arranged along broken stone.

When he looked back up, Belle had disentangled herself from Rob and was swaying down the bank towards the cabin cruiser. She gripped the railings, swinging herself over the side and climbing onto the roof above the cockpit. There she surveyed the bank, her chest swelling impressively as she prepared herself to speak, her belly lean with a ring through the navel, her legs long and tanned beneath the shorts, feet in expensive trainers. The sunlight on her forehead blinded him.

– Hey! she said. There's something I want to say. It's only quick, so listen, yeah…? Check out the house! She pointed at it. Let's never lose this spirit, yeah? Never, never, never! You know what I mean, I know you do. We must never forget about it! No-one forget, or they'll have me to deal with…

A pale impression of the moon was appearing among the trees on the other side of the river, ghostly in the blue of the sky. Belle settled herself on the side of the cabin cruiser, pulling a packet of cigarettes from a pocket and smoking, chewing, swinging her legs. She was dazzling.

It was painful just looking at her.

b: the pilot

It was the last day of summer. Four in the afternoon. In his cupboard of a bedroom, Nick had woken and was slapping his head to rid it of the night before. Between the slaps the house was silent. The windows in the wall in front of him showed a grey featureless sky above the grey featureless Thames. A leaf or two fell almost vertically into the overgrown garden. Another drifted out past the lip of the bank, settling on the water. Nick shivered and pulled a hooded top over the T-shirt he'd slept in. He rifled for cigarettes in a pocket of his combats, hawking and swallowing as he searched through the debris on the floor for a lighter and a hat.

Nick wore a hat devotedly. He had done for months. First there was the bald spot – soon a monk-like tonsure – then the fact that his head, when shaved, looked remarkably like that of a tortoise, as it did now. These days there was the heat-loss issue too. The house was freezing, always. Even on a day as still as this, draughts found their way around the metal window-frames, skirting the bits of newspaper squeezed into every crack and mustering into breezes. Nick cursed to himself as he peered among ashtrays, underpants, textbooks stained in bongwater, beercans, desiccated toast and tape cases, until finally he found a half-full forgotten box of matches, and a moneybag containing skunk.

Nick looked at the skunk. He removed a cigarette from behind his ear and lit it, distractedly. With his right hand he picked up a fishing hat and put it on his head. He'd been determined not to smoke today – just for a few hours while he went to see his dad in Clapton.

He opened the neck of the moneybag and pressed it to his nose, inhaling luxuriously.

– Ohh… he said.

Before turning towards the door, Nick picked up a few pills wrapped in clingfilm. He stuffed them, together with the moneybag, beneath the elastic of his left sock.

The landing and main stairwell of the house faced away from the river: towards the yard, Tim's Nissan, Pete's ambulance, the wilderness of the shrubbery and suburban Kingston. Overhead, a plane was dropping towards Heathrow, a blur of noise which melted, gradually, into the purr of a car on the road outside, then the pop of chippings as it turned into the yard.

Looking through the window, Nick froze. It wasn't that the car – a navy-blue Astra – was particularly strange, but Nick knew it like a mouse knows the wind from a passing barn owl. Inch by inch, he lowered himself to the floor, goggling at the glass, the view becoming yellow-brown treetops and the greyness of the sky.

It was only then that he heard Pete's singing at the other end of the landing. A light Middlesbrough accent, tuneless:

– *I won't let the sun go down on me…*

Nick's eyes snapped from the window. A car door slammed in the yard. Water slapped peacefully against the side of the bathtub. He whimpered, looking momentarily back through the window before scurrying insect-like towards the bathroom door.

– Pete! he hissed. Pete! Pete, get out! Get out! The pigs are here!

The singing stopped. The doorbell played the *Neighbours* theme tune in the stairwell.

14

– This is a drill, right? said Pete.

– Pete, it's them! It's fucking them!

Inspector Hooey rocked on his heels, flattening out his suit with the palms of his hands and inspecting the house before him. By and large he liked this part of the city. He liked the mahogany gates and the double glazing. He liked the speed bumps and the rows of neat little cars with months to go on their tax discs. The house before him, though, didn't really fit into this general picture. His eyes ran over crumbling brickwork, single-glazed windows in peeling metal frames, plant life smothering the walls and most of the roof.

– Hmmm, he said, disapprovingly.

Turning back towards the car, he nodded at the driver, who scrambled out onto the chippings, standing erect by his door while the other two constables coaxed the prisoner to his feet.

– Che cazzo! said Paolo, from beneath his ramshackle Afro. Figlio di puttana!

– Mr Alkalai, said Hooey patiently. We've been through this, haven't we?

The prisoner growled, but his earlier bravado had all but evaporated. His swarthy skin was tinged with grey.

Hooey stroked his moustache, then picked a piece of egg from between his teeth, which he ate. Looking again at the house he saw a head appear quickly in an upstairs window. It was pale, with a fishing hat, rings around its eyes and an expression of absolute horror.

– Exhibit A, he murmured to himself.

– Sir? said one of constables, stepping forward.

– Nothing... said Hooey, then added, Can you keep an eye on the windows, please? If anyone tries to run for it, yell. Okay?

15

Nick hated himself when he was frightened. He hated his hands for shaking, his breath for trembling, his chin for shrinking back into his neck.

It wasn't as if he hadn't had training for this sort of thing. At his dad's it had been quite a regular event: the policemen trooping into the lounge while his dad leant, smoking, against a wall in the hall. One of his earliest memories was watching round his bedroom door while the flat was being ransacked. He'd been wearing Batman pyjamas at the time. He remembered wetting himself, the soaked material clinging to his legs.

– Do you understand? Hooey repeated.

– Huh? said Nick, blinking. I mean, yeah…

The inspector on the doormat was tall, with a moustache, an overgrowing flat-top and a tartan sweater, shirt collars poking from its neck. Behind him, Paolo was in handcuffs, surrounded by constables in uniforms and helmets. His clothes were grubby and his skin was the same colour as the walls.

– Well then? Are any of your cohabitants here?

– Er, yeah! said Nick, remembering. Yeah, Pete's upstairs, in the bath.

– Pete… said Hooey, looking down a list of names. Cleopatra?

– No, Nick faltered. No, that's Belle. It's… Well, actually Pete doesn't live here, officially. He lives in the ambulance, in the yard.

16 Hooey nodded and inspected the three constables now wading across the living-room: ashtrays, newspapers, wine bottles, unwashed crockery, cushions, endless copies of *British Empire* magazine. They reminded him of children, hunting for crayfish in rock pools.

Pete splashed a bit of water on his face and pulled himself reluctantly to his feet, stepping naked onto the filthy pink carpet and looking around him for a towel. He could hear a voice through the bathroom floor: deep, regular, obviously quoting. Nick was answering in syllables, obsequious-sounding. Which was a bit peculiar, now Pete came to think of it. What with his dad and everything, you really would have thought he'd be used to this sort of thing by now.

The bathroom was pink, with a delta of mould on the wall where the watertank had leaked in the attic. Small piles of clothes and towels lay scattered in the corners, but they were dirty, and damp, so Pete took Belle's dressing-gown down from the back of the door – her monogram on one of the pockets – and dried himself with that, then pulled it on. Cleopatra Isobel Armitstead, he thought as he set out onto the landing. What kind of name was that, anyway?

A procession was working its way up from the living-room, Paolo at its head, in handcuffs and denim flares. Then came a pair of constables, Nick, in a fishing hat, his hands stuffed awkwardly in the pockets of his combats, then yet another constable. They passed Pete in silence, without making eye-contact.

Halfway down, the stairs turned a ninety-degree corner and headed into the living-room. A man in a tartan jumper was leaning against a desk near the front door, leafing through a file.

– Mr... Parsons? said Inspector Hooey.

– Hello, said Pete.

– Hello, said Hooey. My name is Inspector Hooey. I have to inform you that we have a warrant to search these premises, obtained under Section 18 of the Police and Criminal Evidence Act.

– Right, said Pete, nodding. What happened?

– Mr Alkalai was found in possession of certain controlled substances, this morning, in Ladbroke Grove.

– Ah, said Pete.

– In a communal house of this kind, this means that we can search the rooms of those residents who are themselves present. Your friend Mr Carshaw, however, informs me that you are not in fact a resident, but a visitor. Is this correct?

– Er... Pete picked up a rizla and a packet of tobacco from the arm of the sofa and began to roll a cigarette. Well, I live in the yard, in the ambulance.

Hooey inhaled slowly.

– Ye-es, he said. Well, Mr Parsons, we do not have a procedure for dealing with ambulances. And, to be frank, this experience is depressing enough already. So I'm going to save us both some trouble, okay?

Pete licked the gum and stuck down the rizla.

– Okay, he said.

– Is there an LSD factory in there?

Pete hesitated, then frowned and looked at him sideways.

– You're joking, he said. Right?

– No, said Hooey. Yes or no?

– No... said Pete, frowning. Should there be?

Hooey made a short note in his file.

– No, he said, there should not. However, we have received intelligence that someone in this locality is running an LSD factory, and seeing as how your friend – Mr Alkalai – was carrying quite a selection of proscribed substances... He cleared his throat. It seemed appropriate to check. Having seen the condition of your house, however, I'm surprised you seem capable of running a bath.

Inspector Hooey smiled mirthlessly and returned to making notes.

Fay often walked back along the river: it was the concreteness of Kingston, it got into her bones. The university was about two miles away, beyond the town centre with its shopping malls and one-way traffic system, adverts and twenty-four-hour garages. There weren't even that many people about at this time of day. Nothing to abate the concrete and the endlessly flickering lights.

The river restored a bit of a sense of balance to things. It flowed between the car parks and the kitsch little houses squeezed along its banks, reflecting the world back off itself – dark and inscrutable, constant where the house in Burnell Road was falling apart.

Angus had been the first to leave, moving away to some cottage in Wales after only a few weeks. Then Rob had gone too, declaring that he was off to Amsterdam to straighten his head out; except that he'd got busted in France, and was now serving seven months in Dunkirk Prison for smuggling. None of which would have mattered that much if Katy had still been there, holding them all together.

But Katy had left as well. The last Fay had seen of her, she was hunched in the back of a car in the yard while her mother went patiently round the house, collecting her clothes and her books. She'd been pregnant, for an agonised fortnight, slipping between despair and short, weird highs when she'd scribble out lists of names; then, without even telling Fay, she'd gone off one morning and had an abortion. After that, all her hopes for the house had seemed to collapse. She'd withdrawn into a silence, as if there'd been nothing worth responding to any more.

Now there were only six of them left.

Belle was leaning against the fence at the end of the garden when Fay got back. She was looking at the river, smoking, and didn't seem to notice her till she was pretty much beside her.

– Oh… she said, when she did. Hello.

– Hello, said Fay.

Belle looked incongruous outside. She'd barely moved off the sofa since Angus left and Rob disappeared to Amsterdam. She was smoking mechanically: slim and curvaceous, effortlessly sexy, her blonde hair tied up high on the back of her head.

Fay had never quite known how to deal with Belle. Katy had had a talent for it – fussing over her, revelling in selecting compliments – but whenever Fay tried anything similar it sounded insincere, or even sardonic. It seemed safer to stick to questions.

– What are you up to? she asked, stopping and pulling her long grey coat tight around her.

– Thinking, said Belle. I think I've been wasting too much energy... On battles.

– Battles? Fay repeated.

Belle sucked on her cigarette, inspecting the ranks of streetlights on the opposite bank.

– Internal battles... I have limited energy resources. I thought perhaps the river would help me recharge.

– It always works for me, said Fay.

– I've been standing here for hours, said Belle.

Fay looked at her: pink cardigan, skintight hipsters. She was shivering noticeably.

– Are you coming in now, then? she said.

Belle said nothing, but she threw the rest of the cigarette in the river and followed as Fay squeezed through the jammed-ajar gate at the end of the garden, weaving through the bushes and setting off across the lawn.

The house was dark, except for the flicker of the television in the French windows. Orange reflected from the slates on the roof. Another set of windows on the left led from the patio into Fay's bedroom.

– Hi, said Fay, opening the door into the living-room, depositing her files on the bed.

Belle left a trail of wet footprints on the clean green carpet.

– Alright, said Pete.

He and Nick were sitting at either end of the sofa. Tim was crouching on the floor to their left, rolling a joint a foot long. The room was murky with smoke and darkness, the faces pale in the light from the television. Belle slumped on the middle of the sofa, winding an arm around Pete.

– You came back then? he said.

– Yeah, said Belle.

– Well, that's something... He fell silent.

Fay turned on the light beside her bed, took off her coat and hung it on the back of the door. She put some trip-hop quietly on the stereo, then crossed the carpet to a small sink in the corner, and turned on the hot water.

– Er... Fay? said Pete, through the door.

– Yeah, said Fay. She dipped a hand in the water and turned on a bit of cold.

– You couldn't come in here for a minute, could you?

Fay crossed back to the living-room and sat on the bottom stair.

– Has Paolo not turned up yet? she asked, frowning.

– Er, no... said Pete. That's what I've got to tell you about. The... Look, the house was raided this afternoon, yeah? About... two and a half hours ago. I thought yous ought to know.

– Oh, said Fay.

A cloud of skunk and menthol tobacco smoke was issuing from the end of the sofa.

– Yeah, said Pete. They'd busted Paolo, but it's no big deal. Honestly. He's okay.

– Where is he, then? said Belle. If it's no big deal.

– No, look, said Pete. Don't worry about it. He twisted the stud in his lower lip. He only had bits and pieces on him,

21

nothing major. They've probably just got him in for questioning or something…

Belle was starting to cry. Fay could see the tears on her eyeballs, reflecting tiny televisions.

– Why us?! said Belle. It's always fucking us! What the hell did we ever do?

The tears turned into streaks on her cheeks.

– Come on, Belle, said Pete. He patted her head awkwardly. I mean, it could have been worse. The pigs reckoned someone in Kingston's running an acid factory. You know? Imagine if it was us! If they'd found one in the potting shed or under the stairs or some bloody place! I mean, we'd all be doing twenty years. Wouldn't we?

– Something like that, Nick muttered.

He received the joint off Tim.

Fay returned into her room, testing the water with her fingers and rubbing off the condensation on the mirror. For a moment she looked at the reflection of her face, pale like the moon, hair hanging limply to either side of it; then she wet her hands and picked up the soap.

c: the sky about to rain

Angus was sitting in his kitchen, wrapped in several jumpers, looking at a piece of paper with *the pilot* written in biro at its top. Across the room a woodburner was spluttering on the too-wet firewood that he'd scavenged from round the stream. It had been the same for days: the rain horizontal on the hillsides, scouring them of leaves and sheep, coming in packs against the pre-war windows, oozing through the cracks in the single-brick timber-framed walls.

Things were closing in on him, that was how it felt. The weather, the autumn, the loneliness; but beyond all those the crippling, swollen brilliance in his head – the burning – that had arrived with Belle, and now spelt her absence. After three or so months alone in a Welsh cottage, Angus had hoped it might have died back down, even slightly; but the truth was that the burning was growing. It was huger than ever: orange towards the centre, cherry red at its edges. Even vodka could barely allay it.

That was why Angus had decided to write. It was the only channel he could think of. In itself, the burning was dazzling, unconfrontable. But if he could only control it, direct it, expose it to some kind of understanding; perhaps then he might still re-emerge.

Angus poured himself another vodka, tucked up his legs underneath him and looked again at his piece of paper. The edges were starting to curl with the damp. The light from the windows was dim and greyish.

So where did the story start? Angus drank the vodka, struggling to think. Then it came to him. The Emperor's broadcast: the end of the Empire. Oita airfield, Kyushu, Japan. August 15th 1945.

Surrender.

– …state of calamity… here to our loyal subjects proclaim… We, Imperial Domain ruler, do… acceptance do instruct that notification be announced…

The speaker shrieked with static: waves of it without obvious amplitude, wiping out words and mangling sentences.

– …continuation of hostilities can only finally lead to our nation's destruction… to die on the battlefield… we must resign ourselves to occupation to prevent our whole people from falling prey to untimely death… concern for the bereaved families must accept… kofuku suru.

Surrender.

And that was it. The Voice of the Sacred Crane melted back into unadorned static.

In the hut, not a word was spoken. Six men sat in rows before the radio, their uniforms identical: goggles on flying helmets, harnesses over issue shirts, clocks in perfect synchrony. Around the walls, the ground staff were arrayed like waxworks, pressed to the shrapnel-spattered walls as if trying to stop the wind that moaned through the holes. Still no-one spoke.

Perhaps we were alike, the six of us. The storm outside was the storm of static was the storm in the mind, and ultimately it all had only one meaning. That is to say, the

unthinkable. All I had known in my twenty-year life was that
we – the Empire – were invincible.

It was the point from which the world emerged.

– Never! cried a voice at last. Never have I felt such
shame!

– Revenge! called another. We must exact revenge!

We had, of course, all heard of the Vice-Admiral's
intention. We knew that the enemy fleet lay west of
Okinawa, anchored: arrogant in its victory. We knew that
we were to fly and fall upon them, dropping like cherry
blossoms.

But as the first man rose from his seat to lead us to the
airfield, such knowledge slipped away from me. It was as if
I had met with a juncture: a boiling point that had, in one
sense, been approaching over minutes and, in another, over
my entire life – an emptiness that had risen and risen, and
finally consumed.

We filed neatly from the hut, discarding our flying helmets,
marching through the wind towards the command pit and
binding hachimakis around our heads.

And crossing the runway, falling into line outside the pit,
it was as if our devastated unit had been subject to a renewal.
The expressions that passed before me were ones of wonder
and animation – red-disk suns glaring from their foreheads
– not pallid with defeat, but urgent, on the threshold of
achievement.

I stood erect, looking blankly across the airfield – the
bomb-pocked, wind-scoured summer grass, the scurrying
engineers – towards the bullet-riddled Zeroes in which we
were to die.

The Vice-Admiral approached slowly. His car was a large
model: black, and in unusually good repair. We watched it
creeping from among the trees beyond the runway, a stray

25

bolt of sunlight flashing from its surface as it rounded the fighters and drew up on the concrete twenty metres away.

The Zeroes were running now, their engines roaring and their propellers sending skewed waves of motion across the field beneath their wheels. The Lieutenant emerged hurriedly from the command pit, hastening ahead of his staff and, nervously, coming to attention outside the car's rear door. A chauffeur then climbed efficiently from his seat, closing his own door and opening the one behind it.

The man who rose to his feet before our line was round-faced, a little overweight and devoid of regalia. His staff – four of them – were similarly without ornament. They flanked him in outfits all but identical to his own; yet it remained the Vice-Admiral on whom we were focused. He looked at the six of us with unconcealed emotion, tears welling and glinting in the corners of his eyes.

– Commander, he barked finally. The order must be given for three planes!

The Lieutenant stiffened. His cheeks were fiery.

– While our Commander-in-Chief intends to launch a special attack himself, he replied, shouting against the wind and the bellow of the Zeroes, we cannot stand aside and see only four planes despatched! My unit wishes to accompany him at full strength!

The Vice-Admiral looked again from the first of us to the last, his presence a light in our midst. He detached himself from his aides and strode towards us, mounting the damaged stand that lay perhaps half the distance between our two groups.

– Will every one of you go with me? he asked.

In unison the six of us raised our right hands towards the clouds, answering:

– Yes, sir!

The Vice-Admiral bowed his head in respect.
– Then I thank you all, he said.

Angus stopped. His head was reeling and he pulled himself up from his chair, wanting suddenly to be outside.

The cottage's door faced west, away from the stream and out across a stubble-coated field that someone would probably have ploughed by now if it hadn't been for the recent rain. Above the skyline of the nearest ridge – above the balding silhouettes of trees – the nub of Llandefalle was a spot of black against the chaos of the sunset.

The rain had stopped; the puddles in the field gleamed like holes in the hillside.

Angus stumbled out onto the lawn, the too-heavy oak door pondering ajar a moment behind him, then gathering speed and slamming shut. Up in the roofspace, the resident squirrels awoke in a panic, chasing across their flimsy plasterboard floor towards the hole beside the chimney. One after another they burst from the eaves, shinning down the climbing rose and hurrying away into the bushes. It was the same every time he went outside. The nerves of squirrels never seemed to steel.

Angus leant on a fence post, breathing haltingly and keeping his eyes on the colours above the horizon. Behind him, the swollen stream grazed the belly of the footbridge. In his mind was Belle; always Belle. Everything he'd ever wanted. He was thinking of a weekend in Norfolk, driving up to the Wash at lowest tide, chasing across the gleaming mudflats, vaulting the river channels till the coastline faded. The sky had been blue, the day had been beautiful. He remembered her running towards one of the channels, springing from the bank, the look that had crossed her face as she realised she wouldn't make it.

27

She'd had an innocent sheen about her – standing up to her thighs in muddy water – a look of disbelief like she hadn't quite believed that falling in was possible. Her arms were frozen above her head, her jeans darkening as the water spread up them; then her T-shirt began to turn transparent.

Up on the bank, Angus was reaching out to grab her hands when a separate idea occurred to him. Belle was looking up at him. The burning flared exquisitely in his mind: clear and brilliant, the sun as you would know it. So he jumped down in there with her, peeling off the T-shirt and his own, peeling off her jeans.

They'd been muddy enough as it was.

d: boiling point

Jaundiced light was leaking between the curtains: a liquid yellowy-orangeness, moving with the lashing of the rain. There were cars caught in lines across the river, the drivers peering through wipers and streetlights in the fading hope of seeing their supper. Some way to the north – the scene of the accident – a couple of buildings were flashing blue. The reflection on the river bristled them with raindrops.

Nick turned from the window, sighing and relighting his joint. He looked at Paolo, who was on the bed, talking, then at the pictures from the Pirelli calendar stuck all over the walls. They'd been all over his walls till he'd started going out with Sonia and had had to get rid of them. Typical of Paolo to fish them out of the bin.

Laetitia Casta! There she was! Partly concealed by Paolo's basil plant, but beautiful as ever. Her long wavy hair, her dreamy dark eyes, her innocent alluring face, her see-through top. She had breasts that proved the existence of God... And then there was that blonde, the one on the wall above the bed! Her big blue eyes and tiny rubber shorts, arms folded coyly across her chest. Paolo had been claiming for about three months now that he'd slept with her one night in Florence. He knew for sure who she was – he said – because just before dragging him off to a hotel for a night of reciprocal passion she'd shown him her passport. Nick had never exactly been convinced by this story, but after three months of Paolo going on about it he wasn't exactly unconvinced either. Paolo had even gone so far as to stick a gold star in the picture's bottom right-hand corner.

Vidi, vici, veni…

But how come Paolo had got himself a double bed?! And a little balcony overlooking the river! And no hydrangea blocking the window. Nick felt resentment welling up in him. There was hardly a draught in Paolo's room. In fact, it was so warm he could have taken off his woolly hat, if he'd only had the energy. It was the raid yesterday that had done it – the raid yesterday and every other bloody disaster of the past three months. They'd drained him. It was all he could do to take another puff on the spliff.

– So, we say that's the plan, said Paolo. I'll ring Steve and get it over with. You go upstairs and check the equipment… Nick?

– Huh? said Nick. That blonde, he thought, the one in the little rubber shorts! Could it really be true?

– Vaffanculo, Nick! Wake up!

– Huh? said Nick again, looking down from the picture. But suddenly someone was knocking on the door and Paolo flopped back on his bed, exasperated, winding a tuft of hair round his ring finger.

– Nick? called Sonia. Her voice was muffled. Nick, you've been in there for ages! When are you coming back downstairs?

30   – Oh, for fuck's sake, Nick muttered. He pulled himself away from the windowsill, slapping himself twice across the face to straighten out and handing the joint to Paolo. Sonia! he told the identical buxom twins stuck to the door. I told you, we've got some stuff to sort out. We'll be down as soon as we're ready. Alright?

– What stuff? said Sonia. Why can't I come in?

– You can't, said Nick, thinking a second. It's… a surprise.

– What kind of surprise? said Sonia dubiously.

– Look, we'll just be five minutes! said Nick. For God's sake, Sonn, go back downstairs, will you?

The sound of aggrieved footsteps receded down the landing. Paolo drummed his fingers on his chest. Nick picked up his flick-knife from the windowsill, toying with it, admiring the blade. On the muted television beside the bed, a healthy-looking Paul Eddington approached from the top left-hand corner, a spring in his step and a twinkle in his eye. Felicity Kendal looked up from her vegetable patch and greeted him with a smile that could have saved the Titanic. The two of them embarked on a jovial conversation.

– Nick, said Paolo. Put the knife away. You are not street-fighting, or whatever the hell you think you get up to. We are in a hole, okay? And if you'd done anything you were supposed to while I was away we wouldn't be in it. So listen. I'm going to phone Steve and make sure he can live with the delay. You know what you've got to do, so, for fuck's sake, can you just do it!

Nick put the knife down, rubbed his eyeballs carefully with the first finger on each hand, then picked the knife back up again, weighing it thoughtfully. He looked at the photos on top of the television: Paolo with a smaller Afro and various – how was it possible? – extremely attractive women.

– Here's what I'll do, he said eventually, his voice calm, confidently East End. First off, I'll smoke that spliff. Then, when that's done, I'll go downstairs and see Sonia. Then – when I'm ready – I'll go upstairs and get on with the shit. Alright? And I'm absolutely fucked if, today of all days, I'm going to start panicking about anything.

– Porca... puttana, said Paolo to himself, shaking his head. Porca fucking puttana.

– And, *infatti*, I do know a thing or two about streetfighting. So why don't you just watch it?

31

– I really must, said Paolo sarcastically.

He reached for the mobile phone on the table beside the bed and dialled in a number. Nick kicked a heap of dirty clothing to one side, took the joint from Paolo, relit it a second time, sat on the floor and turned his eyes to the television. Felicity Kendal – bell-bottoms and Wellington boots – was now smiling sunnily at an indignant Penelope Keith.

Sitting on the edge of the bed, Paolo continued to twist his hair abstractedly. He listened to the sound of ringing in the earpiece for ten to fifteen seconds, then kicked off his trainers and swung his legs up onto the bed, feet vanishing inside blue denim flares as he bent his knees and shuffled a few things aside to get comfortable.

– Steve? he said suddenly. Alright, it's Paolo... Yeah. Yeah. Not that bad. You know... Well, yeah, I mean, that's what I wanted to talk to you about. Not, of course... No. Sure... No. Ha ha!

Nick ceased to pay attention. He took a final puff from the joint and doused it in a half-full tea cup, sinking back against a pile of dirty washing, which made a crunching noise. Reaching behind him, he pulled out one of Paolo's old seafood cookery books and one of the packets of tagliatelle that his mother posted him regularly from Rome. Nick decided to see if he could work out what the writing meant.

32   – Ah, Paolo was saying. No, look, that's what I wanted to talk to you about. We're having one or two little problems... No, nothing major. It's just, well, I just spent a couple of days in the cells. Just got out... No, no. Nothing's been screwed up or anything, but I am going to need, like, three more days till everything's ready... Yeah. No, no. Sure Steve. Vaffanculo! I know you've got people to satisfy... Really, man. No, really, I am sorry. There was nothing I could do... Però, Steve, I can't just produce a million out of thin air, huh! It was, like, a

spotcheck. I mean, on the fucking street. They came back and tore the house apart and...

There was a pause in the monologue. Paolo had returned to sitting on the side of the bed and had his head resting on his right hand. Someone was climbing the stairs. The banisters were rattling.

– Porcoddue, Steve! It was tight! The pigs even told us they were looking for an... A factory!... I don't know. They'd got themselves some tip-off about it... Of course I didn't say anything, man. You think I'm going to show them the attic?... No... No, Steve, hang on! No, no, no, no. Come on, man, this is straight up, I wouldn't do that to you... Steve? Porca Madonna! For fuck's sake, man, come on!

– Look, you bastard! called Sonia through the plyflush. I came all the way over here to see you. If you don't...

– Sonia, shut the fuck up! said Paolo, his hand over the mouthpiece. Steve! Steve, are you there?

– How dare you talk to me like that!

– Sonia! Nick pulled himself to his feet, spreading a part-rolled joint across the floor, colliding heavily with Paolo, who had jumped up to stop him leaving.

– Steve? Steve, come on! Paolo was almost shouting now. Steve, where the fuck are you?! Sonia! Jesus! Tu' madre è una troia bocchinara!

– Right, that's it! said Sonia. The door received a wood-shattering kick. That's fucking it! Goodbye! I'm leaving!

Paolo was standing with his back to the door, one hand still holding the mobile phone, the other on his cheek where Nick's shoulder had caught him. His breathing was shaky. His face was getting paler.

– Sorry, said Nick. I didn't mean...

– Nick, said Paolo. He closed his eyes, then opened them again, focusing with difficulty. Nick, we're going to have to get out of here.

He let his hand fall to his side, revealing a swelling cheekbone, dark already against the rest of his face.

– What? said Nick. What happened?!

– What happened... said Paolo, is we are fucked. The pigs must have been tapping Steve's phone. How else could they have known there was an acid factory in Kingston, and not known where? Nick... Steve thinks we've set him up! I mean, Steve fucking Fisk thinks we've set him up!

Nick stared. He put both hands on his hat.

– But what's even worse, Paolo was whimpering now. Man, we can't ditch the acid, and the pigs are going to be here any fucking minute! They'll tear the fucking house apart! They'll do everyone for it! I mean, we've got to get, like, fucking everyone, and everything, out of here in fifteen minutes or we are...

Nick nodded blankly. A nose of drool had appeared in the corner of his mouth and was setting a course towards his chin.

– You can get the equipment apart and into the ambulance in seven, said Paolo. Yeah?

– Er, yeah, said Nick. The drool was starting to dangle. Where... Where the fuck do we go?

34   – Wherever, said Paolo. It doesn't matter. Just make sure no-one sees you, yeah? I'll pack us a bag, and... try and move the others.

By the time Paolo had picked up his phone and wallet, put on his shoes and tied back his hair, the ladder was down on the landing and Nick was pulling his feet through the trapdoor into the attic, closing it behind him.

With the trapdoor sealed, the attic was absolutely lightless. Nick – crouching on the floor – fumbled to his right, and a second later the prismatic roofspace was bathed with a faint red glow. He had an icy kind of fear in his stomach, the kind he used to get during raids at his dad's. For a second he gripped his temples, trying to pull himself together.

In front of him were a metal case, a sports bag, a small cool-box with knobs on its lid, a malformed tent and four flasks, each with a handwritten label: KOH, HCl, $POCl_3$ and NH_4OH.

Nick reached into the sports bag and pulled on a pair of rubber gloves, opening the case and quickly sliding the flasks into their places, bundling away the lightproof tent and its frame into the sports bag.

Exposed on the floor were a retort stand, an empty chromatography column and a single flask swaddled in tin-foil. Nick packed the column into the case's final space; then he put the stand in the sports bag and turned to the flask. It was the only part of the operation that he approached with obvious delicacy. The flask contained a mixture of benzene, alumina, ethanol, methanol, alcoholic potassium hydroxide and d-lysergic acid diethylamide.

LSD.

A hundred thousand trips' worth.

It was in the last stages of purification, but touch a drop of it and you'd proceed directly into orbit. So Nick lowered the flask slowly into the cool-box with the others, fastening a strap around its neck.

e: something in the attic

The Vice-Admiral stepped down from the stand, shaking hands calmly with his four staff officers and bidding them each farewell. This done, he took from one of them a fluttering length of white cloth.

With the hachimaki bound around his head, the Vice-Admiral seemed to quicken, and his spirit slipped from the officers, becoming as one of ours. For a moment he watched us – the sun of the Empire like a third eye – then he turned and led the way towards the waiting airplanes.

In turn, the staff officers, the Lieutenant and the attendant officials began to weep. Some way inside me a residual instinct of my own was triggered by their emotion, but attempting to glance at one of them I found – somehow without surprise – that my head was unresponsive. It was frozen in the horizontal plane: not unrelaxed, but stopped, as if I had simply forgotten how to move it.

Perhaps this disability had been with me for minutes, perhaps hours or even days without my knowledge. But it seemed to me that the Vice-Admiral's question and my reply – an exchange of only the most distant and detached kind – had brought it suddenly into focus.

I walked towards the Zeroes mechanically, scaling the side of my airplane without a look or a hitch.

Reaching above my head, I felt for the canopy and sealed it. My feet fell automatically upon the pedals. With one hand, I gripped the joystick between my legs and, with the *other, I activated the radio equipment. The coarse fabric covering the control panel left no sense of friction on my fingers. Looking up, I saw the Vice-Admiral wave inside his cockpit, then open the throttle and accelerate into the headwind.*

We followed in order, fighting the weight of the bombs; until finally there was only one of us left, bounding over the patches and holes in the concrete and peering through the strobic blades of the propeller.

– You are God's already! said a voice within my head, and the nose twitched up from the ground, then fell, then twitched again with conviction and led away upwards to the colorless clouds and sky: the sudden flickering emptiness, like the space at the end of a newsreel.

Angus picked up the piece of paper, curved it lengthways and allowed it to fall into the box beside him. Rain and sunshine were coming alternately down the valley. It was around midday, and Angus still had a hangover; but his writing was happening easily and, for once, it made the world seem slightly less inimical.

He left the cottage deliberately, pulling on a coat and setting off across the footbridge, up the opposite bank and over the fields to the track that led to the main road. For ten minutes or so he walked between hedges; then he arrived at a gateway, and stood beneath a tree on the roadside, his thumb held out, repeating a pop song in his head to keep from thinking.

Hay-on-Wye was small, perched on the English border, with a castle in its middle and a multitude of second-hand bookshops. Angus walked through the town nervously, his head down, avoiding eye-contact and ducking into a newsagent. He bought four large pads of A4 paper, which the shop in the village didn't sell, a pocket-sized notepad and a couple of biros.

Leaving the newsagent, Angus paused outside a bookshop with windows lined in yellow plastic and a few withering novels. The relief that had propelled him from the cottage had all but evaporated now – the burning was reasserting itself – but Angus pushed open the door anyway and left his carrier bag wordlessly with the lady at the desk inside.

Towards the back of the shop, a small square room had the word *History* above its door, and Angus entered it, squatting down to inspect the shelves on the left. It was here, on his one previous journey from the village, that Angus had found the diary of Vice-Admiral Matome Ugaki – Head of the Kamikaze Corps. He hadn't really known what he was looking for at the time, except that it had somehow to evoke the same feeling as the burning did. He'd had an image in his mind, of falling from a great height, of the earth below him: a visible, inevitable fate. He'd read a few pages of the diary, and felt his first surge of passion since leaving Kingston.

Looking at the shelves now, though, it wasn't just that there was nothing new there to arrest him. The titles themselves had become somehow meaningless. Angus retrieved his carrier bag and hurried back out of the shop, heading along the high street past a dozen other bookshops, preparing himself to hitch back.

38

The cottage was brick, half-timbered, and buried in the bottom of a valley, concealed by trees from the nearest farm. It had no road, no phone, no electricity, mice, squirrels, a chemical toilet, a chaise longue and a cold water tap. Its owners called it Hollow Cottage, and it smelt like a damp chapel.

Angus drank two glasses of vodka when he got back, quickly, slouched on the chaise longue, the rain beating against the window beside him. He read through the passage he'd written earlier, but the Vice-Admiral, the Zeroes, even the Empire, had now become meaningless too.

He poured himself another glass of vodka, and sat there drinking it, trying to work out where the story went next, trying to ignore himself and blot out the cottage around him.

f: katharine d'aragó

Some way back upstream, Staines bestrode the Thames: a place of car parks, chainstores, middle-income families and retired early-evening television presenters. It was a miracle of uninvention. An attractive curl in a not-unattractive river, girded round – for God alone knew what reason – in architecture of such tacky and intrusive kinds that all its positive qualities were totally effaced.

Beneath the bridges, teenagers with spray cans found themselves unable to think of anything to write. They looked out into the rain, searching for inspiration, and ended up releasing their canisters into the air – finding some temporary satisfaction in the cloud of colour that surged away on the wind.

Canada geese specked with fluorescent paint glided upstream, heads held high, dowdy offspring trailing in their wake. They paddled past the gin palaces moored against the banks, blind to the pedestrians rushing past traffic squeezed beneath umbrellas, to the people hurrying late into the cinema, to the Goths in their Friday night timewarp, to the Sainsbury's now closing for the evening.

Inspector Hooey knew little about Goths, gin palaces, or what was on in the cinema, but he did know that Sainsbury's was closing and was in a reasonable mood, having made it there before it did. Bleary through the wipers and the splashing rain, the lights ahead of him changed down to green. He released the handbrake and let his Fiat Punto roll forward another few feet.

Enfopol – Hooey's destination – was a slightly secret estab-
lishment, as opposed to a top-secret one. A lot of things about
Enfopol were slightly done, the most notable of which being,
probably, its disguise as a soft-toy factory named Playtime's™.
What with funding restrictions and other crippling expenses,
there were just seven soft toys on the premises and only earnest,
besuited people ever went in and out of the gates. Anyone
looking must immediately have been suspicious, which was one
of the reasons why the Enfopol headquarters were located in
Knowle Green, where people didn't tend to look.

In theory at least, Enfopol was a good deal more sinister
than its appearance suggested. At some point during the early
1990s, the FBI – with all the discretion you'd hope for from
such a noted team of dark horses – started to lobby the
European Council of Ministers to install a surveillance network
equivalent to their own Echelon. That is to say, a computer
system capable of capturing and analysing every phone call, fax,
email or telex from anywhere to anywhere else in the entire
world. Some protested that this was an excessive kind of
precaution, but the FBI did not seem to think so. As they
observed in one of their nudging communications to the
European Ministers, there was serious and organised crime to be
combated – a level of specificity they were never to surpass –
and that meant Europe getting an up-to-the-minute real-time
digital tapping system, able to locate the origin and destination
of any call anywhere within seconds, even to translate what was
being said from an almost boundless number of languages into
English, French, German, Japanese or Finnish – Finland being
the source of the necessary equipment.

Needless to say, Enfopol tended not to work properly, and
even when it did the march of technology meant that any
decent encryption software could flummox it in slightly less
than a second; a fact, presumably, of which a criminal of any

41

sort of seriousness or organisation would have been more than aware. All the same, Enfopol had come into existence. The European Council of Ministers had given its approval, bypassing all other European and national governments, and now – in the British division, at least – MI5 and the CID were collaboratively having to deal with it. Meanwhile, the conspiracy theorists of the Western world were tearing their hair out with a concern that closely resembled delight.

Playtime's™ soft-toy factory was at the end of a cul-de-sac named Sykes Lane. The semi-detached houses lining the rest of the street were silent, the occasional rectangle of a television visible through their drawn lace curtains. Hooey passed them slowly, turning left at the gates to the industrial estate and arriving at a barrier, beside which a well-lit guard was slumbering in a cubicle. Arching above him were ten pictures of different-coloured tumbling cubes, each displaying a different letter, which together made up the word *PLAYTIME'S*. An eleventh, smaller cube reading ™ was partly obscured by a bush.

Over a period of about three seconds, the guard woke, focused, pretended to recognise Hooey and pressed the button to raise the barrier. He saluted and remained conspicuously awake until Hooey had parked his car against the wall near the main entrance, taken his briefcase from the passenger seat, draped his raincoat over his head and dashed through the rain towards the shelter of the lobby. Then he went back to sleep.

Inside the entrance, a skinny, red-haired receptionist was talking to the telephone on matters plainly not related to her job. Pot plants were arrayed on small stands around the walls. In a final bid to maintain the Playtime's impression, a number of catalogues from major toy stores had been heaped on a coffee table beside an IKEA sofa. Large, mysterious soft toys with no indication as to what they were supposed to be sat on presentation tables between the pot plants. A corridor led away –

straight, white and shrinking. On either side of it were doors marked with individual letters.

– Tell you what, Dave, said the receptionist, I'll ring you back in a minute. Yeah… Yeah. He he he! Yeah. Okay. Ciao!

She hung up the phone and turned to the tall moustachioed figure beyond the desk.

– What can I do for you? she asked, fixing him with unnatural blue contact lenses.

– I'm looking for a… Norman Teather, said Hooey.

– Well, we've only got the one. The receptionist giggled. I'm afraid we're going to be needing him.

– I had an appointment at eight, said Hooey sourly.

– F, said the receptionist. She leant forward over the desk and pointed a self-manicured finger down the corridor, then picked the phone back up from its cradle and pressed Redial on the bank of buttons in front of her.

The corridor descended through most of the alphabet before a sign finally announced the letter F. The door in question was blank and white as everything else was. Hooey knocked, then pushed the door open.

Before a line of aerodynamically shaped computer monitors, a balding man with an unfortunate sweep to his hair was sipping at a cup of tea. His free hand held a mouse. As the door opened he turned unhurriedly towards it.

– Hooey, said the man, a small smile appearing on his lips.

43

– Teather, said Hooey. He held the look for two or three seconds. It seems to be, er… later than when I last saw you.

– It does, agreed Teather. It does indeed… Moustaches are still in, though, I see. Will you have a seat?

Hooey rolled a chair from beneath a desk, across the lime-green fitted carpet, and sat without comment. An air conditioner-cum-heater was purring in a distant corner, behind the dozen or so empty desks that filled the room. Teather was wearing a Playtime's™ identity badge on the lapel of his suit. It featured a photo of himself imposed on a heap of varicoloured soft toys.

– ITMA, said Teather eventually. Remember ITMA? That crackly old record you had?

– So I put the baby on the butcher's block, Hooey quoted instantly. What did you say?

– I said: What's a plenipotentiary? Teather responded. I mean… He repeated the quote in a bad Liverpool accent, then began chuckling to himself. Hooey, he said. Hooey, and good old ITMA!

– So here you are, said Hooey, almost smiling. Behind this desk. Of all the people for me to wind up working with… All the bloody people.

– And you a pig! Teather observed in disbelief. You! Hooey! Of all people. A filthy rozzer!

– Look here, baldilocks, said Hooey, running a hand through his own thick hair. What are you precisely? A stuffer of soft toys?!

– A spy! said Teather, his chubby face looking pleased with itself. Your actual bona fide MI5 spy!

– Are you hell, scoffed Hooey. You're a pig with pretensions, neither more nor less. Which is even bloody lower than I am.

– Ooh, it gets personal! said Teather, rising from his seat and walking towards a drinks-maker patterned with tannin that was leaning against a wall. You want tea?

– Coffee? asked Hooey.

– You're even a clichéd pig! said Teather. No. You cannot have coffee. Coffee's banned from Room F. You can have tea, or soup.

– Alright, tea.

Teather returned to his seat with two paper cups, in each of which was a sickly white liquid with a strip of aluminium

44

sticking out of it, revolving slowly, looking like a magnesium fuse.

– Cheers, said Hooey sarcastically. So…?

– So, Teather echoed.

– So, what do you get up to in this wretched bloody place?

– Come, said Teather. I'll show you.

He rolled his chair sideways across the lime-green carpet, making space for Hooey before the wall of monitors. Then he put a hand on the mouse, dispelling a screensaver that read CAN I DO YOU NOW, SIR? and bringing a hundred or so options onto the central screen.

As he was running the cursor down the list, the sound of ringing burst from speakers on either side of the desk.

– Kofi! said a voice. Alright, it's Jeremy.

– Alright Jeremy, said another, moodier voice. What you after?

– Any chance you could do us for an 'enry, mate?

Teather clicked a Mute option on the right-hand side of the screen.

– Okay, he went on. This computer has the capacity to trace any sort of electronic communication anywhere in the world. Well, that's the theory. We're having a bit of trouble right now with anything outside western Europe, and the time-lag's terrible. Two, three minutes once it's been through the translator, locator and all the other shit. No-one can work out why it's taking so long. Anyhow, most of what I get to deal with is useless East End drugdealers talking in slang… I mean, like dope, you know? Hash. They used to just say Henry for an eighth of an ounce. Nice and simple. Henry the Eighth, you know. These days I'm getting Anne Boleyns, Annes of Cleves, Catherine Parrs… I even had a Solitaire one time. You know, Jane Seymour: Solitaire in *Live and Let Die*. Jane Seymour: third wife of Henry the Eighth. Took me about two hours to

45

figure that one out. I mean, all this equipment at your fingertips – billions of pounds of it – and you spend most of your time trying to work out what the fuck cockneys are on about.

– So, what about that call just now? said Hooey.

– It's just automatic, said Teather. It does that with loads of numbers. A team works here, each with a shortlist of a few thousand criminals – er, suspected criminals, rather – corresponding to one particular area. All of them get recorded. A few of them we actually get the machine to tell us about as the call happens… In here we do London. Drugs mainly, but you know how it is. People will pursue other lines of enterprise. Take that bloke Kofi, for instance. He's always just been a regular dealer but we reckon he might be moving into shipments before long, out of Morocco and the 'dam. Hidden in soft toys, perversely enough. There's even some signs he might be shifting old IRA weapons. It's the decommissioning thing. There's a good few people trying to get rid of stuff…

Teather leant back in his chair, picked the tea bag out of his cup and threw it into the waste-paper basket, leaving a trail of tea-drops across the whitewashed walls.

– Anyway, said Teather. That call just now? Here's Kofi, and… here's where he is.

A photograph appeared on the screen. In its middle a tall mostly-black man was getting out of a beige Ford Escort with the curry houses of Brick Lane in soft focus in the background. To the left of him, a detailed map of the Bethnal Green area showed a small red light moving south down Brady Street, east down Darling Row, stopping at the junction with Cambridge Heath Road.

– Mobile phones, Teather continued. Aren't they fucking marvellous? Firing out microwaves the whole time. People are paying to be tagged! Paying for it!

He was about to go on when a light blinking beside a name on a left-hand screen brought him suddenly alert. He swung the cursor across the screen and reclicked the Mute option. Instantly the sound of ringing appeared in the speakers.

– It's Steveyboy, Teather muttered. You know him? Right bastard. Steve Fisk?

– Steve? said Hooey. Do I know Steve?! I've been on this Steve Fisk business since the start of it.

– No shit? said Teather, starting to drum his nails against the table. By the way, we're listening to a recording. For some reason it's had to go through the translator – it's automatic – so it's like two, three, four minutes old. I don't know.

Finally the ringing stopped and, after a slight pause, a foreign – Italian – voice spoke a little nervously from the speakers.

– Steve?

– Yeah. A thicker, South London voice.

– Alright, it's Paolo…

– Ah, Paolo! The voice became suddenly more affable. How you doing?

– Shit! said Hooey, excitement rising in his stomach. I don't believe it!

On the two central screens, a pair of maps had appeared. One showed a flashing yellow light: a landline off Coldharbour Lane in Brixton. The other showed a flashing red light: a mobile beside the river in Kingston.

– Yeah. No, no, the Italian was saying. Sure Steve. Vaffanculo! I know you've got people to satisfy…

On the furthest screen to the right, the words GO AWAY AND PERFORM SEXUAL INTERCOURSE UPON YOURSELF had appeared in throbbing green capitals, which were halfway through fading back into black when they were replaced by the word BUT.

– You are failing to understand me, said Steve. His voice had returned to its earlier rasp. I need you to meet the schedule.

47

– Porcoddue, Steve! Paolo exclaimed. The words GOD IS A PIG burst onto the screen in the same lurid green. It was tight! The pigs even told us they were looking for an… A factory!... You think I'm going to show them the attic?

– I don't fucking believe it! said Hooey. The attic! They fucking had it! Teather, get your coat! We have an appointment in Kingston.

There was a crack as Steve slammed down his phone, and the ensuing torrent of Italian and English tumbled into emptiness. The words THE VIRGIN MARY IS A PIG – followed shortly by YOUR MOTHER IS A FEMALE PORCINE FELLATRIX – leapt gleefully onto the screen. In their green, pulsing light, Room F sank into silence.

g: having a dream,
i will go up in the sky

– Right. Okay, listen! said Paolo, almost arriving in the living-room but pausing on the second stair to maintain presence.

No-one moved. On the sofa, Belle was smoking a joint she'd been smoking for some minutes. Pete was slumped beside her, dozing. Tim was kneeling before a rizla, a bag of skunk, a box of matches and a menthol cigarette. On the television – as ever, the only source of light in the room – Richard Briers was running across a field, escaping from a climactic incident involving a goat.

Paolo felt suddenly as if he were looking into a nest of some kind, as if the room was a deliberate construction and not just knee-deep in filth after all. Pete, Tim and Belle were hibernating in their chosen element: a spilt ashtray, a broken personal stereo, an Indian drape, an empty Spar whisky bottle, a styrofoam box from McDonald's. How the hell was he going to get these people to move?!

He'd run through various possibilities upstairs – packing everything, waiting for Nick to finish in the attic – but most of them were utterly incredible, and obviously there was no way he could tell them what had actually happened.

– What's up? said Pete, raising his left eyelid.

– Er... said Paolo. Look, yeah? I don't want to worry you or anything, but, well... we're going to have to get out of here.

– What? said Pete.

– What happened to your face, Paolo? said Belle, talking round her thumb, looking up from her pink fluffy cardigan.

Credits were unfurling on the television. The bruise on Paolo's cheek had darkened, the rest of his face so white now that a beige colour seemed to be welling from beneath it.

– Oh… Nothing, said Paolo. It's not important.

– It looks quite important, said Belle.

– For fuck's sake, said Paolo. Listen to me! There's no easy way to say this, but… The pigs are coming! Okay? We've got to go!

There was a pause.

Belle's thumb was hanging from her mouth. Tim was looking up from his joint, staring across the room at him, his face cadaverous in the black-and-white light of an advert.

– Huh?! he grunted.

– You're joking? said Pete, receiving the end of the joint from Belle. Right?

– I swear to God, said Paolo. Man. They're going to be here any minute!

– Fuck! said Tim in a croak and staggered to his feet, stumbling through the rubbish towards the stairs. Oh fuck!

– No, no, said Pete. Hang on. Paolo, how exactly do you know this? You've been in your bedroom for the past half an hour.

Tim hesitated, looking round him confusedly.

Before the bust, Paolo had never really known what it was like to be scared. It just wasn't something he did. Paolo relaxed, and designated; and if his mother wasn't around to be obedient then the chances were that someone else was. He was a closed-ranks group-member Roman. It was an inviolable condition. Even on four microdots lost in Elephant and Castle with half an ounce of skunk down his underpants, he'd never been worse than wasted.

Now he was completely terrified.

– What's going on? said Fay, through the door to her room.

50

There was a squeak of springs, and the sound of a book being dropped on the bedside table.

– You're wasted, right? said Pete. Paolo? You're tripping or something?

– I'm not fucking tripping! said Paolo. I'm totally fucking straight! Look! He glanced right as Fay appeared in the doorway to her bedroom, then flicked on the living-room light. Look at me! I swear to God, we have not got time for this! I was talking to Dave on the phone. He's supposed to be coming round to get some pills and an ounce off me, but the phone was still on when we finished talking – Nick was passing me a joint – and I heard a police radio down it, in the background! Someone reading out my name and our address! Nick heard it too! Just fucking ask him! It said some other stuff about a traffic accident... They took my number down on Wednesday! I swear to God, you've got to believe me!

6 Burnell Road was so much the nicest place Nick had ever lived, he was quite unable to explain why he found it so unpleasant. Even the leaking ceilings and concrete stairwells at his dad's in Clapton had something homely about them: football in the car park, car stereos in the lounge, people he knew in the next-door flats. A sense of life, if nothing else. Creeping past the kitchen window, into the yard, the house beside him seemed somehow menacing and lifeless at the same time – like the statue of a crouching predator, its flanks all streaked with birdshit.

Nick stashed the case and the cool-box out of the rain beneath the ambulance's back bumper and pressed at the rubber-coated button that stuck from the right-hand door. He swung himself inside immediately, throwing Pete's futon, clothes and scattered bedding out of the way and scrabbling at the catch that

51

undid the spare-wheel compartment. It was a procedure that he'd run through two or three times before when no-one was about. The compartment's lid fell back against a heap of books. Nick reached down into the hole and, pressing his left hand against the floor, hoisted the wheel up from its socket. Clinging to the tyre, he climbed back down into the yard.

The shed was in a corner beneath a copper beech, sagging like a wet cardboard box. Inside were three non-functional lawnmowers, tangled in a heap. Cunningly tangled, in fact. With the wheel rolled into place behind them, you would never have known it was there.

Escape! That was the thing! Getting the hell out of there! Nick realised suddenly that he was far more excited than he was frightened by the prospect. A clean break from this endless downwards slithering. He'd never been anywhere west of Swindon before. It had to be better than your average night in.

Trickles that smelt of wet wool were streaming from Nick's hat. As he ran back to the ambulance, he pulled it off his head and hurled it through the open doors, into the cab, where it hit the inside of the windscreen with a splat. He installed the cool-box carefully in the wheel's cavity – lying it on its side – and stood the case upright in the remaining space at the end. Then he closed the lid and started to rearrange the bedclothes.

There was a torrent of water spilling from the gutter about halfway round the side of the house – two feet of it shimmering in the light from the kitchen window. Nick barely faltered as he ran down the path. He flattened his skinny body against the wall and swung himself round the frame of the garden door, onto the bottom of the poky back stairs that led towards his room.

Under the unshaded light the living-room no longer looked much like a nest. It looked, in fact, very much like what it was:

a disgusting tangle of magazines, clingfilm, records, collapsed furniture and mouldering food. On the sofa, Belle and Pete were squinting, their eyes glassy and bloodshot. Fay was standing bemusedly in the doorway to her room, her face shining its moonlike white, in a blue fleece and grey trousers low on her hips.

From behind the sofa Tim had just produced a large lockable moneybox, and was arranging piles of twenty-pound notes inside it, and a large number of bags full of pills, weed and cocaine.

– Jesus... said Fay, staring.

– Tim? said Pete, leaning forward to look at it, coiling his dreadlocks into a shape like a pineapple on top of his head.

– Okay, said Fay, after a pause. That does look pretty dodgy.

– It's alright. Tim headed into the kitchen to fetch some acid from the fridge. The police need a separate warrant to get into a box with a lock on it.

– You sure? said Fay.

– Well, I don't know if you've noticed, said Paolo, but I've got a fucking court case coming up. If the pigs show up, they will tear this place apart! Tim'll go straight down and, after Wednesday, so'll me and Nick. The rest of you'll get done for possession at the very least. Probably assisting dealing or something too. I mean, think about it! End of house! Prison! Parents...!

The banisters were rattling in the stairwell. Belle was perched on the edge of the sofa, her eyes so wide now you could see the whites right round her irises.

– But... she said. I mean, what on earth would they say?!

– Hey, said Nick, appearing on the stairs with a heap of blankets and a sports bag slung across his back. You lot coming, or what?

– Shit! said Belle. Shit!

She jumped up and sprang – surprisingly lithely – towards the stairs. Fay turned, and vanished back into her room. A

53

moment later there was the sound of the sink filling, then the splashing of hands and the thud of the soap as it dropped back into its dish.

– Pete, said Paolo. We can't risk it.

Pete sighed. He pulled himself to his feet.

– I don't know, he said. I'm wrecked, but… I mean, you're not about to make something like that up, are you?

– We're going to have to go in the ambulance. We'll never fit in Tim's car. Like, if we can just get out of the road…?

Nick pulled the front door open quietly, slinking outside. Pete took his wallet from the arm of the sofa and pushed it into a pocket of his jeans, blinking, his forehead lined horizontally.

– Like, he said. But there isn't any more to this than what you've just been saying, is there? I mean, I'm not trying to accuse you of anything, but it does all sound a bit weird.

– Pete, said Paolo. I've had about two minutes longer to process it than you have. We've just got to get out of here, okay?

With a roar the ambulance's three-litre engine burst into an approximation of life. It choked and coughed to itself, stationary beneath the drizzle-haloed streetlights, exhaust drifting off down Burnell Road.

54

Paolo and Nick were slumped breathlessly against the back bumper. In the cab, Bob Dylan was singing *Talking World War Three Blues*. Fay was sifting through the tape bag, nudging the accelerator to keep the engine going.

– Oh fuck, muttered Nick, dragging himself to his feet and setting off back down the road. Wallet!

A hundred yards away, Tim, Pete and Belle had just emerged from the gateway. Tim was reeling, his arms wrapped around his moneybox. Pete had a hand on his shoulder. Belle was bowed beneath an enormous bag. Paolo watched her as the three of them got closer: the sway of her hips, the swell of her breasts against her cardigan.

He was starting to feel back in control of himself, confident even. All the seeds that he needed were there. Now he just had to hang back a bit and let the others piece it all together.

The chippings ground loudly as Nick hurried across the yard, covering his chest pocket with his hands to keep it from the mizzle. Bounding into shelter on the doorstep, he removed a folded sheet of paper, checking behind him for anyone watching before slipping it securely into the metal frame that was screwed to the front of the door.

As he skirted the puddles on the way back through the gateway, Nick became aware of distant police sirens. They were somewhere south, coming up through Kingston. Dozens of them, it sounded like, fused into a single unearthly wail, building by the second.

He was sprinting by the time he arrived back on Burnell Road. His hat sparkled with water droplets. On either side of him, Toyotas were parked in shadows and prefabricated balconies stuck from detached pebble-dashed gables. The sirens were really getting loud. Ahead, the ambulance was rumbling quietly to itself, its brake lights staining the wet tarmac. The engine was idling more evenly now, its underused cylinders starting to find a rhythm.

– Woh! said Fay, her head half out of the passenger window.
  – What? said Pete.
  – Where the hell are we going? said Belle.

– I just saw Sonia! said Fay. Back there, between the street-lights!

– Wh…? said Nick.

– Don't stop! said Paolo. Pete! Just get in the next road!

Pete swung the steering-wheel anticlockwise and the ambulance lumbered out onto Richmond Road, accelerating slowly, the wipers whining on the windscreen. He flipped down the indicator.

– Christ, Pete! said Fay. Come on, we can't…

She hesitated. In the wing mirror, a platoon of police cars was appearing up Richmond Road, swamped in traffic, flashing and wailing. A grey Fiat Punto, several squad cars and a van were indicating as Pete spun the wheel and turned down Lauderdale Lane.

He exhaled slowly, parking the ambulance in an unlit corner, pulling a cigarette from his pocket while continuing to coax the accelerator.

– They were all after us?! said Fay.

Blue light was glancing from the houses beside them.

– Well, said Pete, through a mouthful of smoke. That does kind of change things… So what the hell do we do now?

– Man, said Paolo. I only know what I told you. He paused a moment. But, we can't exactly go to Dave's, can we? I mean, it's only a little flat and the pigs'll have his number now anyway. Under the circumstances, I don't think there's anyone else in Kingston who'd put all six of us up…

– Which means? said Pete.

– Angus's? said Fay.

Her expression had become more serious. Her eyes were on the light in the trees and on the houses.

– No! said Belle from the back. No, we can't go and see Angus. I mean… Fuck! We can't!

– He's the only person we all know who isn't locked up.

– Well, said Paolo. I can't think what else we're going to do. Seeing as how half a dozen police cars are parked around our house.

– Fuck's sake... said Pete. You weren't talking about sarin or anything, were you, Paolo?

– You know the way, Pete? said Nick.

Pete rubbed his temples with the tips of his fingers.

– Look, he said, Angus lives miles away. I'm stoned, and there's a very good chance that he won't want to see us.

– He definitely won't want to see me, said Belle.

– But we don't have much choice, do we? said Fay. And no-one's seen Angus for months. I mean, it's mushroom season about now, isn't it? You never know, we might quite enjoy it.

She glanced over her shoulder.

– Mushrooms?! said Tim, a moment later.

Pete finished the cigarette and released the handbrake, letting the ambulance roll cautiously back towards Richmond Road – peering both ways for police cars – and accelerating between semi-detached facades, lines of balding oaks, evergreen hedges, all-night garages, parkland, sports grounds and phone-boxes.

Overhead, the breeze was tearing holes in the clouds' orange awning.

57

h: another lunatic plan

Six little airplanes, gleaming in the afternoon sun. When I next came back into focus, they were there before me – stumpy machines with bulbous noses – configuring at the four kilometre cruising height and setting a course for the south.

The spacing between each of us had an accuracy I felt certain that we had never achieved before. We banked in unison to starboard, the Earth appearing suddenly beside us with a level at 75 degrees to our own: the distant blue arc of the Pacific horizon, the surprising green of Kyushu with mountains, rivers, forests and, perhaps in a second as the Zeroes righted, the cinders of Nagasaki spread across the western coast. We passed through walls of white – cumuli, altocumuli, cumulonimbi – into leaden blindness and out again suddenly into sunlight, every time in the same exact formation. Being the last, I could see these things.

Finally, the target was becoming an actuality. This was the dream that had dangled before us all since infanthood. Not the

Sergeant Major, barking, erect and elegant in the training yard:

– Pain and pity will make men of you!

Not the boots and the fists, but the glorious consummation of the samurai. The sacrifice. The place in Yasukuni: pantheon of the Gods. Except – facing it now through flickering propeller blades – this too was grown insubstantial. It was the dream, and that was all it was: an after-image lingering in the air, torn apart and for the first time exposed to interpretation.

To my uncomprehending eyes it now seemed a barrage of questions, out of which I found one rising into prominence: Who, or what, had volunteered for this insane enterprise?

For whom were we giving ourselves, if not the Emperor? Did even the commanders know? And, of all that Radio Tokyo had told us over the last twenty years, was this too without basis? Had the foreign infidel ever even planned to bayonet our babies? And what of the A-bombs, that the Vice-Admiral had so humbly deemed Wonders?

I was, of course, no more able to answer — even to confront — these questions than I was to turn my head. The only answers were questions in themselves, in their turn prompting more questions: a chain reaction of their own.

Again the formation was passing through clouds, and for some minutes we were lost to everything but the occasional glimpse of another plane. Re-emerging, however, we were configured as precisely as we had been when we first came together. Seven Zeroes between cloudbanks, the bombs in place of ventral drop-tanks like progeny in some early stage of gestation.

The radio had been silent for some time now — since indeed the climb from Oita — but here between cloudbanks static resumed suddenly in my ears, bringing in a rush the memory of surrender. For a moment it continued, then a voice began talking: the pilot of the plane behind the Vice-Admiral's.

— Vice-Admiral! he exclaimed. A cylinder has exploded! I cannot remain airborne!

The plane had started to shiver noticeably just before the voice appeared on the radio, and smoke was spouting from beneath the left-hand 7.7mm machine gun.

— Alas! he went on. I must return to Oita!

The airplane departed our formation as if it had thrown a hook into the passing world and been plucked away into *reality. My eyes turned upwards to follow it as it banked, its engine screaming. Neither the Vice-Admiral nor anyone else offered any comment. The spaces between us were not compensated through any kind of reformation. The mission continued, rigid as ever in its design.*

Glancing around, Angus realised suddenly how dark it had become. He had no idea what time it was, but the lingering grey streaks of cloud above Llandefalle were stained red along the edges and the vacant spaces of sky were so pale they were barely blue. Inside – by contrast – it was now so lightless it was all he could do to make out the woodburner, far less the hand-scrawled words he'd been writing moments earlier. Closing nights were getting to be a serious problem. He was practically going to have to start hibernating soon.

– Oh Lord! said Angus, picking up the vodka bottle, rising and heading towards the door.

As ever there was no-one around outside. Except for a fortnightly appearance by the redoubtable Mrs Lloyd – checking to see if he was still alive – Angus had only ever had one visitor: Pete, his best mate, who had turned up one night two and a half months earlier, having driven down from Middlesbrough. Actually, a rambler had stopped and leant on the fence behind him one time as well, when he was chopping wood; but the sound of his voice had alarmed Angus so much that he'd missed the log and nearly caused them both an injury. So the rambler had run away.

– Coca-colonisation! Angus yelled randomly at the darkening sky.

It was a curious thing. The longer Angus spent in isolation, the less he felt distinct from his immediate environment. He was, of course, talking to himself, but he was definitely directing his remarks at separate objects. In the absence of anyone to define himself against, the stream seemed as much a part of him as the nape of his neck, as the squirrels were in the roofspace, as the wart was on the back of his left-hand thumb. It wasn't that he felt himself especially At One with everything, just that the need to differentiate and assert himself had somehow waned.

– Amphetamine-annexation! he addressed the footbridge.

– Amyl nitrate-appropriation! he told the elder tree.

Angus tipped up the vodka bottle, filling his mouth and swallowing, steadying himself against the elder tree as the numbness spread outwards through his stomach.

He was having to drink a lot now, when he finished writing. Where the story might be helping him – shoring up his own feeble structure: alcohol, weather, meals and squirrels – when he re-emerged from it, he felt as weak and vulnerable as he did when he woke in the mornings.

– Ecstasy-expropriation! said Angus to the fence that divided his garden from the field.

He turned and went back into the kitchen, picking up the two twisted, blackened old kettles from the flagstones beside the woodburner and carrying them through to the little side room to fill them with water. First the larger one, then the smaller. Then he took both of them back to the woodburner, placing them on the hotplate before opening the door at the front and – careful to avoid disturbing the baked potato – restoking the fire with a few choice pieces of wood. Such was his routine.

Such were the threads of his web.

Crossing back to the other side of the room, Angus took two candles down from his dwindling supply, stuck them into a pair of tasteless floral candlesticks and lit both with one match, then picked up one in each hand. At once their reflection came back at him from one of the countless mirrors arranged around the walls. He moved the candles about till the shadows allowed a fair impression of his face, then he slipped one next to the other between his right-hand fingers, leaving his left hand free.

Angus's hair was a mop-like mess – shaved about four months earlier – and he pressed it back from his forehead, holding it there to inspect himself. His face looked gaunt: thinner than it should have done, with clumps of stubble on his cheeks and chin and a frown mark starting between his eyebrows. He was good-looking, though. His nose and jaw had a preciseness about them that looked quite dignified in some lights, and did at least offset some of the hair. His eyes looked back at him – pale blue and open-looking – the reflected flame of the candle shining from just below his pupils.

Burning, in his eyes and in his mind.

A mouse squealed in the bottom of the woodstack.

i: would that i had seven lives to give for my country!

Sonia started jogging as she turned off Richmond Road, pulling her hood down over her face to try and keep the drizzle out of her hair. Feeling for the openings, she buried her hands back in the pouch above her stomach. Her head was bowed. Her mouth was set with purpose, moving in and out of shadow as she hurried beneath the regular streetlights.

Perhaps Nick really had had a surprise for her – something wonderful – and she'd only stormed out because of what Paolo had said. It was a possibility. Not much of one, admittedly, but one she wanted so much to be true she could scarcely bear it. For two or three minutes she'd been stared at by her solid, glossy white front door, the rain running down it in strands, before eventually realising she was just going to have to go back and sort things out. It was all Paolo's fault. It was always Paolo's fault. Every time she and Nick had problems, there he was, lurking around in the background.

63

Sonia had gone a good way down Burnell Road, her eyes on the glistening pavement, when the sudden roar of an engine made her look up. A decommissioned ambulance very much like Pete's was rolling down the street towards her. She hesitated between streetlights – jeans slit an inch at the ankles, trainers ragged, hair sandy, headlight-illuminated eyes wide and brown – and, momentarily, she saw Fay looking back at her from the passenger window, her face waking with recognition.

– Hey! shouted Sonia. Hey!

But the ambulance rolled on towards the junction, pulling away briskly into the traffic: car horns and, not far away, the squall of police sirens. Strange. So far as she knew, no-one had been anywhere in Pete's ambulance for months. She'd have to ask the others when she got to the house.

Sonia resumed jogging, jumping the puddles spread across the gateway and landed, breathing heavily, on the doorstep to number six. Light filtered through the door's frosted glass. She pulled her hood off, shook out her hair, and pressed the doorbell.

Through the hiss of the drizzle, the police sirens were now becoming deafening. Blue was throbbing in the trees near the end of Burnell Road. Sonia was reaching up to re-press the doorbell when suddenly she noticed a scrap of paper jammed into the metal grille beside it. It had been put there in a hurry and, on it, in almost-illegible capitals, was her name.

The sirens stopped, more or less simultaneously. With the splash of wheels in puddles, cars were pulling into the yard behind her, their engines cutting out.

SONN, said the note. WE'VE HAD TO GO TO ANGS. WE'RE IN SHIT BIGTIME. WHATEVER YOU DO, DON'T TELL ANYONE YEAH? PLEASE! I LOVE YOU, SONN. I SWEAR TO GOD I'LL MAKE THIS UP. NICK. (I LOVE YOU).

64   Sonia stared at it for a second, scrambled with emotions, her hands shivering; then, carefully, she raised it up over her stomach and chest and pressed it into her mouth, chewing until it was pulped enough to go down her throat. Around her shadow, the glass was glinting blue.

– What the hell's she up to? Teather whispered, leaning across the roof of the Fiat Punto.

Hooey said nothing. On the doorstep, the girl was finally beginning to turn round, her arms held out awkwardly to either side of her as if she was unsure whether to stick them straight upwards. She was skinny, freckled; pretty almost, in a direct kind of way.

– Do not be alarmed! announced Hooey authoritatively. Do exactly as you are told and everything will be okay!

Sonia blinked a few times, then squinted while her eyes attuned to the lights. The trees hanging bedraggled above the yard were cut in blue pulses from the dirty orange of the sky. A few feet in front of her, a grey Fiat Punto had its headlights on full beam. Its two front doors were open, and behind each, steadily, a man was becoming discernible. The one to the left was tall and stern-faced, with a dated flat-top and a bushy moustache. His left hand was on the roof, holding a mobile phone the size of a brick. The other man was a more haphazard figure: shorter, soggy-faced, crowned with an unfortunate swept-over hairstyle. From the two police cars and the van behind them a stream of black figures was emerging, bent double, scurrying silently down the path to the garden, a couple with rifles clutched to their chests.

– Come down from the step, Hooey instructed. Keep your arms where we can see them.

Sonia complied, her muscles so rigid that her gait was like a zombie's. Around the house, the figures were now crouched regularly behind tree trunks, dustbins, a decomposing grass-roller, parts of the rockery. The rifle barrels were turned towards the front door.

– Wh…? said Sonia. Her voice was tiny in the quietness. Wh… What the hell's going on?

– I am sure, said Hooey, his tone condescending, that you know the answer to that far better than we do.

– I don't! said Sonia. It came out as a bleat. I really don't!

65

I don't even live here!

– If you would be so good as to sit down in here, Hooey continued, pulling open a back door of the Punto, we would like to ask you a few questions...

– But I don't know anything! Sonia protested, looking round desperately, getting in. I mean, how could I? There's not even anyone here! I don't know a thing!

– Well, I think you do, said Hooey, waving an arm in a sideways motion above his head.

At once a twitch of readiness passed across every bush and potential place of concealment as far as Sonia could see. Hooey bent down through the driver's door and reached between the seats. He reappeared holding a sleek black megaphone that might have been modelled on a bugle. This he switched on with a practised flick of the thumb and raised to his lips, directing the bell at the louring bulk of the house. For a moment, the only sound was the water dripping from the eaves.

Hunched on the back seat, squashed against a mound of shopping bags, Sonia was beginning to wonder at the man with the flat-top. She watched his back – the checked high street-casual jumper, the nape's suggestion of a mullet – with a nervousness that was fast becoming perplexity. He reminded her irresistibly of a schoolboy showing off.

– This is the police! Hooey was barking. I repeat, this is the police! The house is surrounded! Come out through the front door with your hands in the air! You cannot escape!

He lowered the megaphone and, carefully, turned the volume up another couple of notches. He then paraphrased what he'd said before.

From behind the vehicles parked in the yard, a team of six men in black bulletproof outfits scampered towards the house – still doubled up – and pressed themselves against the walls on either side of the front door.

Hooey took a loud intake of breath.

– This is your final warning! he told the house. Come out now or we will be forced to bring you out ourselves!

The eaves dripped to themselves for a second or two.

– Very well, said Hooey. Teather, would you mind keeping an eye on this young lady?

– Glad to, said Teather equably. He continued leaning on the car door.

The men pressed against the wall of the house were now so eager they were practically salivating. It took the very slightest nod from Hooey for one to step back and level a kick at the Yale lock, which gave way at once with little more than a splintering noise. One by one the men sprang into the living-room, busily issuing grunted instructions to one another and trampling in boots over piles of ashtrays, saucepans, hip-hop records, crumpled beercans, *British Empire* magazines spilling from maroon binders and the endless other junk that was littering the floor.

Within seconds, three or four others left the bushes to follow them inside, Inspector Hooey leading in chequered jumper and beige slacks. They fanned around the house, taking the front and back stairs two steps at a time, kicking bedroom doors open, lifting the lids of large boxes, ransacking cupboards, peering cautiously under beds, sideboards, sofas and the larger heaps of rubbish, looking behind hot-water tanks, washing machines, chests of drawers and '70s dust-laden curtains.

Hooey realised at once that the house was empty. Not that there'd been any great sense of habitation on his earlier visit, but you got a nose for presence once you'd been doing this sort of thing for long enough, and this was, if ever he'd been in one, an empty house. Now he came to think of it, he'd known it was empty even before that girl had told him so. Partly he'd just sensed it but, if he were to be honest, it was hardly to be

67

wondered at. The whole business of the raid had taken far too long: the traffic, assembling the men, the tap on the phone call.

He'd had to go in, though, obviously. He could hardly have stood around outside with Teather there, smoking nonchalantly. Hooey had had the nickname Bronson when they were at school together, and it was how he still thought of himself. Bronson: the brooding loner, honourable but dangerous. A hell of a good nickname, Hooey reflected, even if it had had more to do with the uncontrollable hair on his upper lip than his fighting prowess. Bronson was the man he wanted Teather to see. The man who went into houses!

By this point, the more zealous officers were scouring the walls for hidden cavities and the garden for a refuge of some sort: an old air-raid shelter, for instance. Hooey was elsewhere, and he didn't attempt to stop them, even to point out that the house had obviously been built some years after the end of the war. Instead he turned his attentions to finding a pole: a line of enquiry which took him down the landing, through two heaps of books, clothes, broken furniture and mould, and finally into the peeling pink-carpeted mess of the bathroom. Where, in a corner, he found a suitable, never-unwrapped mop, which he took back out onto the landing and began prodding at the attic's trapdoor.

68

Even with the two front doors open, the smell of fish in the Fiat Punto was becoming unbearable. The bags beside Sonia were spilling slowly in every direction – upset, presumably, by frenzied cornering on the road to get there. The nearest, at any rate, contained a number of poorly wrapped packages which were in the process of toppling onto her lap. Sonia suspected they were haddock.

The soggy-faced man now had his arms folded on top of the passenger door and his chin resting on a wrist. He was smoking absently, observing the comings and goings of the gunmen, the crashings around through the big metal-framed ground-floor windows. Occasionally he shifted his weight slightly and glanced back to check that Sonia was still there, though not very often.

Escape crossed Sonia's mind, remotely; except she knew that she'd never be able to walk or do anything practical if she actually tried it. Here she was – captive of the pigs, with her friends and the man she loved in some terrible fucking predicament, their house overrun with gun-wielding lunatics – and she was paralysed by the smell of fish.

Eventually it was too much. With shaking hands Sonia gathered the carrier bag gingerly by the handles and swung it over to the other side of the pile. The one beneath began at once to slip sideways, starting to empty newspapers and magazines across the vacated piece of seat. Panic cloyed in Sonia's stomach. It made her want to be sick. The fish smell kept filling the air, choking her.

– Er...

Sonia was starting to cry. She could feel a flood around her eyeballs.

– You alright?

The soggy-faced man was peering over the passenger seat, looking really quite concerned. Blankly Sonia noticed he was wearing the identity badge of a soft-toy factory.

– Why don't you get out for a minute? he suggested. It can't be too much fun in there. Here, have a cigarette, or – er – something... I've got a pack if you want one.

Sonia was too shaken to say anything. Tears were gathered now on her lower eyelids, gleaming in the house lights like eyeball menisci. A second or two later she managed to nod, dumbly, dislodging a couple of droplets, which ran with pent-up speed towards her collar.

Teather walked round the car and opened her door; except as Sonia pulled herself along the seat to get out the heap of bags slid with her. A box of eggs broke open on the floor – followed by a carton of milk and a pouch of processed turkey – then the newspapers and magazines fanned like cards across the seat, some falling into the slime seeping into the floor.

– Oh, fuck, said Sonia miserably.

– Take me from behind! instructed a hugely overweight Indian woman, her naked bosoms clenched between fleshy upper arms. Most of the other magazines said similar sort of things.

– Ah… said Teather uncomfortably, looking in through the door. Perhaps I'd better clear those up. Here, er, you have a cigarette.

He handed her the packet.

Hooey felt abstracted, leaving 6 Burnell Road, waiting for an armoured straggler before turning off the lights and pulling the door closed behind him. It was how he often got after raids: philosophical, introspective. Outside, the last traces of drizzle had cleared now, ushering sparse, faint stars into their place – what few could outshine the streetlights. Hooey stood on the doorstep, looking across the yard, trying to think.

Sometimes he just got swamped by it all. Here he was with this task, to rid the country of illegal drugs; but he hadn't got the resources, and never would have, and no-one in the country – including him – thought that it was possible. It reminded him of a character in a film he'd seen one time: an athlete, training by swimming against a river, staying still for hours on end. Noble, Hooey might have been, but sooner or later the river was going to beat him. He just seemed to get tireder and older, and if you wanted drugs you could still go out and buy them. In the end, it did make you wonder if he was doing anyone much good. Except lawyers, of course, and judges, and drug dealers, and the drug squad itself.

– PC 273, spluttered a radio. Accident on the A310 between Wick Road and Crieff Court is now clear. We are awaiting instructions...

The girl was hunched against the side of Hooey's car, her face bloodless, smoking feverishly. Teather was leaning beside her. He glanced towards the front door.

– Alright, Hooey? he said.

– Hhm, Hooey grunted. Well, they've taken it and spread a load of dust everywhere. I don't think there's anything left to send anyone down with, but the attic's lightproofed and there's a forty-watt dark-red bulb in the socket. For what it's worth. Could be useful.

– Ah, said Teather. Shit.

– And apparently Steve Fisk got away. Took his car. His phone's switched off, and so's that Italian bloke's we've got the number of – Paolo Alkalai – so we've not got any idea where they are, either.

– What have they taken? said Sonia.

– Oh, for God's sake, said Hooey wearily. You know what was in there. I know what was in there. We've got bigger fish to fry than you round here so, look, if you're not going to be nice to us, we will just do you for something, okay? We just want you to cooperate.

Hooey sat on the edge of his driving seat, frowning and trying to concentrate.

– Shit! he said suddenly. Hang on! Just there, where the van was... Of course, there was an ambulance there! An old ambulance! A, er, Transit!

– Er… said Sonia.

– Okay. So what's the registration?

– How the hell…? Sonia's mouth stayed open a moment. I mean, I don't know! Why would I know that?! I don't even know what was supposed to have been in the attic!

– Well, said Hooey, if that's how it's going to be, we're just going to have to begin at the beginning. Aren't we?

He reached mechanically into the glove compartment of the Fiat Punto and pulled out a clipboard with a multiply sub-divided A4 piece of paper on it.

– Name? he said.

– You are skating on very thin ice, young lady, Hooey observed. I'll ask you again: what's the full name of the owner of the ambulance? He looked at Sonia, quivering in the back.

– Peter, er, Parsons, said Sonia miserably.

– Er? echoed Hooey. What's that? An initial?

– No, said Sonia. His middle name's Damien.

Hooey looked at her.

– Okay, he said at last, and picked up the radio handset from its socket on the dashboard. HQ Kingston, come in, HQ Kingston, this is Inspector H. Hooey. Do you receive me?

White noise filled the car, fusing with the smell of warm haddock. Vague through the steamed-up windows, the only other police officers still around were sitting in an Astra a few feet away, listening to pop music, sharing a can of Coke. Teather was standing in the yard on his own, talking to the radio. The phone in his pocket was ringing insistently.

– Hooey, this is HQ, the radio coughed. Receiving you, over.

– HQ, we have one PARSONS – as in… more than one parson – PETER DAMIEN. Twenty-six years of age. Place of birth: Middlesbrough. Try the General Hospital... He is the owner of a decommissioned Ford ambulance, possibly C or D reg. Try anything – insurance records, road tax, vehicle registration, whatever – just get me the licence number. Did you get that, over?

– Copy, Inspector. Over and out.

Hooey sighed and rubbed a hand through his hair.

– Alright, he said. That's it. We know where to find you, so you might as well go there.

Sonia opened her mouth to say something, but closed it again and pulled herself defeatedly along the seat, back into the yard. A single length of inscribed yellow ribbon was draped around the house. It fluttered in the rising breeze. Bits of orange cloud were skipping through the trees.

– Yes, okay, Teather was saying. Okay, I'll get some bread... No, really, I'm on my way back this minute... I know, dear. Yes, it's very important.

For a moment or two, Hooey watched the stars and the nearly-full moon edging its way from the copper beech; then he climbed back into the Punto. The tyres sucked at the ground as it rolled towards the gate.

Sonia reached into a pocket of her jeans for rizlas and tobacco, and, shakily, rolled herself a cigarette for the walk back.

73

j: belle, *or* the burning

Angus was lying on his bed, staring at the ceiling, formulating the next part of his story. He'd given up trying not to about half an hour earlier. It was there, ready, wanting to be written. Upstairs a squirrel was creeping across the roofspace. Outside the moon was working its way northwards, its impression of a small dusty window sliding across the floor towards the chimney.

Finally Angus furled a blanket around his shoulders and went to sit cross-legged on the rug between the bed and the low, small westerly window. The moon was huge, near enough to Llandefalle to throw shadows down the hillside towards him. The top left of its face had a sliver missing – like it had suffered in a minor celestial collision – but its light was quite uniform, like a more manageable form of daylight.

Amami O-shima. Tokuno-shima. Okinoerabu-shima. For some time now the islands had been visible before us, like patches of algae on the smooth curved surface of the Pacific. Now the day had moved on: clearing and ageing. The islands were beneath us. Okinawa lay long and uncertain through the propeller blades, an hour distant, its colors confused by those of the evening.

A spectrum was evolving across the ocean: from the bloody darkness of the east, through Okinawa itself, Ie-jima – where the summit of Akari-Ue might still have seen some trace of

the sun – to the sky-high conflagration in the very corner of
my right eye. From four kilometres' altitude, of course, the
sun remained some way above the horizon. And, while I was
unable to turn towards it myself, for some minutes yet bolts
of light glanced affirmatively from the panes and panels of
the other four aircraft.

It had been a half-hour since the second departure, his fuel
tank bleeding and his bomb for an instant filling the hole in
the configuration as it fell away beneath him. Yet now, even
in the absence of our 250-kilogram burdens, return to Oita
would have been impossible for any one of us. It was a
condition of which we must all, in our separate ways, have
been aware.

I could not say for sure whether the sun and the moon were
opposed. The one had risen without my knowledge, eclipsed
by the other's descent, and invisible besides, my head being
fixed. But it happened suddenly that the plane of the windows
– around 70 degrees – brought images of both into the
cockpit. Pure, if inverted: a sun to the left and a moon to
the right. Both within the field of my eyeballs. Red and white
respectively.

Could it be, I wondered, that every one of us was
witnessing this phenomenon? Our levels and positions being
accurate as ever to one another, it did appear likely. My eyes
grazed across the laden Zeroes passing south between the sun
and the moon, the tiny clouds in the distance haloed in the
day's dying light, and – there, for the first time, off the south-
west tip of Okinawa – I saw Kerama-retto: the enemy,
basking in its victory.

75

The moon was sinking at last behind Llandefalle. Its impression
– Angus's head cut black from the middle – was fading,

shrinking, approaching a point where it would vanish altogether.

He turned back towards the bed, ragged bits of mattress dangling beneath it. Emptiness was flowing cold and heavy in his stomach. If he ran to Llandefalle, he thought, he would see the moon for another few minutes. But the thought of watching it sink again made the emptiness flow more heavily. And besides, he'd have to cross the river.

So Angus refurled the blanket around his shoulders, donned a pair of moccasins with most of the soles missing and headed towards the stairwell.

The stairs were in a tight, steep half-circle spiral. Cobwebs stuck to his hands as he felt his way down, trying not to trip on the blanket, fumbling for a matchbox in the last beams of moonlight that were sneaking through the kitchen window.

The room issued suddenly from the flame, stabilising a little as he transferred it to a candle on the table – a circle of shadow shuddering over books and a three-month-old copy of the *Brecon and Radnor Express*. He picked up the glass and the vodka bottle and carried them over to the woodburner.

The bottle clinked as he set it down on a cold damp flagstone, shimmering reassuringly. For a moment he watched the tiny distorted candle burning inside it, then he removed the cap and filled the glass.

76   – Big Ben, he said, by way of a toast.

Relief fanned instantly through his stomach, diluting Belle or whatever else wasn't down there, deadening the edge of his own refracted burning.

There were embers still glowing at the back of the woodburner, visible through coatings of ash that exploded into clouds when Angus blew on them, breaking into flames as he heaped on newspaper and pieces of the broken pallet that he used for kindling.

He sat cross-legged on the hearth-rug, looking into the fire, allowing words and thoughts to drift until finally they settled on Ipswich: childhood, his family, their neck of the suburbs, their street, their house.

They'd lived in a place with four bedrooms, in a close he'd called Too Close, with a car and a half and a garden with a tree at the end. Too Close was in an arc, its ends drooping towards a junction and a main road. If you had a ball or a toy with wheels, it would always, sooner or later, take off and vanish into the traffic. Angus's stabilised bicycle had once caused a minor pile-up. He'd never quite grasped why this problem hadn't occurred to someone at the design stage.

There were a lot of things Angus had never quite grasped about Too Close. Why anyone lived there was one. Why he lived there was another. For as long as he could remember he'd had this terrible sense of being blinkered, as if incalculable wealth was beyond the drab things around him.

The relief when he left for London was indescribable. London was like a light for him. It was a place of possibility, even if the university he arrived at was as concrete and anodyne as everything he was trying to escape.

NO TUITION FEES! the signs were saying in the halls of residence. NO STUDENT LOANS! EDUCATION FOR EVERYONE!

They were tacked to trees and notice boards, little letters at the bottom instructing people to congregate in Parliament Square on Saturday. Having arranged his concrete cubicle – pinned up his posters and put his dope smokers' techno on the record player – he wasn't really sure what to do next. When he looked outside, everyone somehow seemed to know one another already. His nervousness revived his self-disgust. It was only chancing across Pete in the corner of a bar – twenty-five, dreadlocked, shellshocked – that he wound up knowing anyone at all.

So the two of them found themselves in Parliament Square, cross-legged in the road, streaks of red in Angus's shoulder-length hair, a seamless wall of riot shields around them and Big Ben rearing over the top. There were four hundred or so in the enclosure – ravers, indie types, hip-hoppers – the people, Angus found himself thinking, who still gave a shit!

Then, looking towards some excitement behind him – a couple of people were trying to get out, a fight beginning with a policeman – he saw the most beautiful girl that he'd ever seen in his life: blonde, mascaraed, lissom, curvaceous. Everything!

His mind came alight.

– Alright, Belle? said Pete, turning to see what Angus was looking at. I didn't know you were here.

It was magic! A little shuffling and they were sitting next to each other. A few sentences and they were kissing.

Around them, the protest was splintering, beginning to reveal itself. People were checking their watches against the last train home. Others were braving the clubs, vying for escape. The songs – *Give Peace a Chance* – were rendered verseless, petering too soon.

But it wasn't as if any of it mattered: London, the yearning. All Angus had ever wanted was to reach that light, to find whatever would finally make him complete. And that was Belle, the moment he first saw her: clear and brilliant, to be sailed by and aimed towards.

k: steve

Sonia patted the pockets of her jeans until she heard the clink of her house keys, then pulled herself up from the doorstep. Glancing around, she reached beneath her waistline and rearranged her clinging underwear. Damp and cold seemed to have made it to her skin the entire way down her body. She felt wretched.

There was a car across the road, its lights on and – complicated by shrubbery – what seemed to be two men inside it. Now she came to think of it, the engine was running as well: a cat-like purr audible above the traffic on Richmond Road.

Sonia relit her cigarette. Somehow she couldn't make herself move. She exhaled and thought about Nick, then the ambulance pulling away without her, then the Jaguar, which was still across the road, the passenger door breaking from the panelling.

They were looking at her as they approached: two well-built, deliberate figures with the streetlight throwing shadows across their faces. The one to the left was huge – built and moving like a boxer – the other was about Nick's height, his shape owing more to shoulder pads. Both were wearing jackets, with open-necked shirts and vaguely casual trousers. They stepped indifferently through the puddles in the gateway. Their feet crunched on the chippings.

Sonia looked around her several times. She considered throwing herself round the corner of the house, heading for the garden and making a getaway down the towpath; but both of them were plainly better runners than she would ever be. So Sonia smoked, and couldn't move, and hoped desperately that the men would turn out to be friendly.

– Hello, said the smaller one, stopping in front of her, his hands in his trouser pockets.

The huge one just stood there.

– Er, alright? said Sonia hesitantly.

She held the smouldering cigarette butt in her hand for a few seconds, then threw it awkwardly into the flowerbed.

– Would you mind telling us something? asked the man, without moving.

His hair was outlined against the streetlight: a tidy, parted style with a few bits sticking up towards the back. His accent was South London. His eyes were bulbous, Sonia could see that much.

– Perhaps we could go inside, he suggested.

– Well, like, why? asked Sonia, after a moment. What good would it do?

She looked again from silhouette to silhouette, squinting, becoming aware of her heartbeat – so loud, she couldn't believe that she hadn't heard it earlier.

– Good's not really the issue, the man replied pleasantly. What you're wanting to ask is: What bad would it do if I don't? And, conversely, that's just not the sort of question you'd want us to answer… Mac! he added.

The other man took a couple of steps forward, produced a long thin knife from beneath his jacket and slit the ribbon neatly, letting the two ends flutter away to the ground. He then pressed a hand against the Yale lock, and stood back to watch the door swing open. In a moment, a shaved head, a heavy jaw and close-set eyes found their way onto Sonia's retina.

She stood with difficulty. Her brain felt like tripe. She teetered as she looked towards the men's averted faces, lights in the air around her. Then she felt herself being pushed backwards.

– Okay, said a voice. You can wake the fuck up now.

Sonia remembered herself suddenly and tried to open her eyes, and tried again. She couldn't. She tried to move her arms, but she couldn't move them either. Claustrophobia poured over her. Images of jaws, bulbous and close-set eyes flickered around her brain. Bruises ached the whole way down her spine.

– Aggh! she exclaimed.

Her mouth worked.

– Aaaggh! she exclaimed again.

The sound was small and strangled. It faded back into dripping water in the sink, the huskiness of her own breathing, a pair of heavy feet, passing through newspapers, bottles, ashtrays, treading more evenly on the linoleum in the kitchen.

– You will probably have noticed by now, said the voice, that you can do nothing but breathe. Oh, and make that moaning noise. Now. Assuming that you wish to continue your life doing anything more than that, or for that matter even doing that, you will answer the following questions… One:

– Where the fuck have they gone? said Mac, from the kitchen.

His voice had been deeper – resonant – taking its cue like something from a fucked-up drama.

– How…? managed Sonia. She was whimpering now. How the… I mean, I just came round here to see Nick. He wasn't here. I got grabbed by the pigs and they were all going on about some fucking thing in the attic, and everyone keeps fucking thinking I know everything, and I don't even know what the fuck was in there in the first place! I don't! I swear! I don't fucking know anything!

– Well, said the man behind her. We now know what you told the police. Perhaps you used fewer expletives the first time round, huh? But, you see, we're not the police. We believe that you can do better than that. So, let's start again… One:

– Where the fuck have they gone?

Again the question reverberated in the kitchen, so deep now that Sonia thought she could feel it through the chair.

– Please! Her voice was rising into a wail. All I know is I came back here, and the ambulance was gone, and everyone was fucking gone… and that's it!

– Well, said the man behind her, pleased, we appear to be getting somewhere already. In your eagerness to cooperate, however, you have bypassed what we asked you and answered instead question number two…

– How the fuck did they go there? interjected Mac, who seemed to be rifling through a heap of cutlery.

– …which we hadn't yet got to. Still, we do not hold that against you. You were telling us about the mode of transport. An ambulance, you say? Tell us about this ambulance.

– It's, it's white! said Sonia. White, with like marks where the stickers used to be, and, er, I don't know, maybe it's fifteen years old or something. I think it's a Ford. It just sat in the back of the yard, there! I mean, I never even knew the bloody thing worked!

Sweat was clamming beneath the rag, or T-shirt, or whatever it was that was tied around Sonia's eyes. It ran from her hairline, from her temples, from her eyebrows. The man's head was very close behind her. She could picture its eyes – bulbous, watery even in the half-dark – its thin face, scarring of some sort emerging from the shirt collar. He was starting to make sniffing noises.

– You smell of fish, he said finally. Haddock. It's horrible. Now, listen to me a minute. Yeah?

– Yeah, said Sonia. It came out as a sob.

– I don't think you are fully appreciating the gravity of this situation… Do you feel this?

Something small, cold and hard pressed against her shoulder blade.

– Yeah, said Sonia, in a squeak.

– This is a gun, the man observed. If we have to kill you, we will definitely kill you; but we'll probably just make sure you never walk again or something first. Running, skipping, jumping. Do you like running, skipping, jumping?

– Yeah, squeaked Sonia.

– Okay! said the man. Running, skipping, jumping… What we need now is truth, okay? There are two persons: one Italian Jew named Paolo Alkalai, and a friend of his named Nick, whom I take to be the person that you came here to visit. They have fucked us over and attempted to set us up, which was not to be advised… Now. We don't – of course – want to hurt anyone. He chuckled lightly. The point is this: if you and everyone else does just as they're told, everything will be roses. Running, skipping, jumping. Okay?

Sonia nodded silently, her eyes screwed up beneath their blindfold.

– Where the fuck have they gone?! growled Mac.

His voice was just to her left now, thick with menace. She started to shake uncontrollably.

– Please, she moaned. I just don't know. I just came round and… that's it!

Behind Sonia's head came a crinkling noise like that of a carrier bag; then a hand struck her hard across the face. Warmth flooded from Sonia's crotch, slowing and beginning to cool as it spread around her thighs.

– That, said the voice behind her – steelier now – was, as you probably guessed, your final chance to avoid something very, very horrible happening to you. You can talk now.

83

Sonia was so choked up with panic that nothing issued from her throat but strangled gargling noises: partly sobs and partly insensible wails.

Behind her the plastic crinkled meditatively to itself for ten or fifteen seconds, then in a rush her head was covered, the plastic handles tight around her throat, the tiny bit of air thick with the taste of bag.

– Ngggh! she screamed, muffled, her head thrashing against unmoving arms. Nnngggh!

Her eyelids were turning a rich, bloody red, the sound of her voice growing faint against the pounding of the pulse in her ears. Washes of vagueness were coming and going. Her lungs seemed too big for themselves. Tears were soaking into her blindfold, saliva smearing over her jaw, her lips, her cheeks. Her body convulsed. Suddenly she could only think of her mother, big and sturdy-looking, her hair long and golden, like it hadn't been in fifteen years.

When, in a moment, the saliva and the pumping of Sonia's chest chanced to make a vacuum against the plastic and a balloon came back into her mouth, her teeth gripping it instinctively and tearing it open. In a backwards scream she filled herself with air.

Sonia vomited for about a minute, trying to breathe, choking, fluids going inside the carrier bag, some making it through the hole and spreading themselves across her lap, her legs, the floor and the general filth.

Somewhere above her – distantly – Sonia was aware of voices. She seemed to be horizontal, but she was so detached and floaty-feeling that she really wasn't sure. They were, she thought, the same voices from earlier, but she couldn't understand what they were talking about, and their tone was different too.

They were urgent now, nervous even.

– Look, one was saying. This is the shit, yeah? They know about the connection! They'll screw them for a deal!

There was something sharp pressing against the side of Sonia's head. It seemed strange to her, in conflict with the floatiness. She tried to move to get away from it, but somehow her muscles weren't working properly.

– So we find them. Find them. Grease them. Bury them. Fuck them! Fuck the acid! Don't take any chances... What's the problem, Steve?

Redness was shivering behind the blindfold. Sonia seemed to be coming back to herself; she was starting to taste the vomit in her mouth, feel the pain in her head and her back and the terror in her stomach.

– Alright, said Steve. Wake her up. We'll give her two minutes then we get nasty.

A big hand was slapping Sonia sharply. It took her a few seconds to realise what it was, and when she did she was already coughing, struggling against the ropes, shivering the length of her body.

– Where the fuck are they?! roared someone. You fucking repulsive little bitch!

– Ang's, Sonia whispered through the vomit and the tatters of the carrier bag. They went to Ang's...

– O-kay, said Steve, suddenly calm again and pleased-sounding. Once more, we appear to be getting somewhere. Now then, what is Angs?

Sonia felt herself being hoist upright, the joints of the chair squeaking, the carrier bag being pulled off her head.

– Ang's, Sonia stammered. Ang is Angus. Angus Persey. He... He used to live here... Now, he lives in... Wales, near the Black Mountains. There was just this note for me on the door, saying they'd gone to Ang's and not to tell anyone.

85

– Good, said Steve approvingly. So, let's have a little speci-ficity, shall we? We have a possibly D-reg Ford ambulance containing… how many altogether?

– Six, breathed Sonia.

– Six people, said Steve. Which is currently heading for the Black Mountains in Wales, where they are planning to hole up with some fucker called Angus Persey, who lives in the village-or-town of…?

– I, er, I don't know, said Sonia weakly. I really, really, really don't!

There was a long pause. Somewhere to her left the wheel spun on a lighter. She smelt cigarette smoke. The draught creeping round the doors and windows was beginning to make her go numb at the extremities.

– Now, it strikes me, Steve's voice had hardened again. It strikes me that we already heard that line earlier, and that it wasn't really the whole story.

A metallic click came from her right, and the same hard coldness pressed against her, this time on the wet denim that covered her right knee.

– Do you think we're fucking around here? he asked.

– No, whispered Sonia.

– Do you suppose that I won't blow your kneecap into this filthy disgusting fucking floor if I have to?

86

– No, said Sonia, quieter still.

– Then you suppose right, said Steve.

– Stop! said Sonia. Please! Look, all I know is he lives in a cottage, on his own. It's got no road to it. No electricity. Nothing like that. It's in the Black Mountains, near a place called Hay-on-Wye. It's, er… I don't know. The kind of village or parish or whatever it's in, it's a Welsh word. Someone did say it one time. Two syllables. Please don't shoot me! Please! I – I am trying to remember! I… think the first syllable was, was

Liss. Liss, or something. Liss-something! Liss-pen, or Liss-way, or something. I swear to God I don't know what. If you showed me a map…?

– Liss-something, repeated Steve, rolling the word in his mouth. There was a tension in his voice, underneath the smoothness, you could hear it sometimes. Liss-something. Right. If what you have said is not true, you should speak now. It will be very much for the best, I do assure you… Okay, then. In our car, we have a map. If we find on that map a place called Liss-something somewhere in the Hay-on-Wye locality, we are going to waste no further time and we are going to go there. If we don't, we will come back in here and we will continue from exactly where we left off, except without the charitable approach. Do you understand?

Shivering and coated with vomit, Sonia nodded dumbly, images of the two men's silhouettes hovering in her eyelids – the huge and the thin – their movements charged now with malevolence. From nowhere, she felt hands clasp beneath her, pulling her crotch away from the chair, two other hands delving in her pockets: one removing her wallet, the other her keys and various urine-soaked bits of paper and tissue.

– 12 Fernhill Road, said Steve slowly. Is this where you live?

– Uhh, Sonia affirmed feebly.

– If you've lied to us, he continued, we will come back, and we will kill you. Do you have anything else you want to say?

Heavily, Sonia shook her head.

– No, she mouthed, and felt the handle of some sort of implement being pressed into her hand.

– Good, said Steve, his voice sounding equable again. Now, you are holding a knife that Mac has generously removed from the kitchen for you. If we have not returned in the time it takes you to count – aloud – to, let's say, one thousand and six, you may start using that to try and get away

87

from the chair... Then you may do some running, skipping, jumping. As much as you like, in fact. Okay? There. That wasn't such an ordeal, was it?

l: o darlin'

– So, said Fay a little dubiously, you've never had insurance or tax or anything, on anything, ever?

Pete puckered his lips, thinking.

– Er… yeah, he admitted. I suppose I've not.

– And no-one's ever done you for it? I mean, you've been driving for nine years or something?

– Mmm, eight or nine. Something like that. He took a cigarette from the packet on the seat beside him and tapped its filter a few times against the steering-wheel. Well, it's luck, isn't it? It's like not paying on parking meters. You just need a bit of a streak, then you've saved enough to compensate any fines or whatever.

Pete lit the cigarette, steering with a corner in the road. Fay was smiling; there were shadows beneath her cheekbones.

– So, you saved up the money you would have spent?

– Oh no, said Pete. It's just a principle. Like, obviously, the actual money goes on women and cocaine and islands and that.

Fay's relief on leaving London had hit her like a wave. For the best part of an hour, she'd stared at trees and the occasional passing house in a state of near-bewilderment. A pressure had fallen from the sides of her head, like the walls had fallen from the verges as they rolled out of London. She felt fresh, unconstrained. For the first time in years, she wasn't yearning for anything.

– Fi-fi! mumbled Paolo on the seat between her and Pete. Oh… bella Fifi!

Fay stretched her arms above her head, arching herself between the floor and the seat-back.

– Okay, she said, sitting back down. Who's Fifi?

– Not me, said Pete.

Paolo was snoring erratically, his head lolling back over the seat, jerking upwards as he breathed.

– Fammi un bocchino! he groaned.

– I think he might like her, said Fay, taking a tape from the glove compartment and replacing the old one in the stereo.

– Paolo! said Pete. Hey, Paolo! Who's Fifi?

Paolo opened his eyes painfully, wincing at the bruising on the side of his face. He frowned at the hedges pressing in on either side of them, then at Fay, and finally at Pete.

– What? he managed. What did you call me?

– Who's Fifi? said Pete.

– What's Fifi to you?

– Paolo, you were rolling around moaning Fifi! Bella Fifi! I think we ought to know who she is.

– Oh, that Fifi! said Paolo, apparently reassured. Bella Fifi! My God! Now, she was a woman! You know, she had this thong…

– Not that bloody model! said Fay. She was never called Fifi!

– What's wrong with Fifi?!

– Oh, come on! said Fay. The whole thing's cheesy enough without her being called Fifi as well.

– Excuse me! said Paolo. Fifi is a very respectable name. Infatti, I even have a sister called Fifi.

– Do you? said Pete. And you dream about her?

– Okay, okay, said Paolo. I'm going back to sleep now.

In the back, the air was awash with smoke. The never-repeating breakbeats drifted between the curtains, easy among the debris and the sprawling bodies. On a side-wall, a mad-eyed heavily made-up woman stared down from a poster, snakes in place of her hair. An enormous Indian drape coated the ceiling overhead, falling into folds at the bottom of the opposite wall.

– Are... Are we here? asked an Australian over the music. Are we unique?

Tim sat insensibly a couple of feet from the rear doors, his back against the drape and his eyes turned up to the little windows – awestruck – like they were icons, or glimpses of sky from a prison cell. Now and then he cupped his hands into a makeshift bong – an enormous joint was pressed between two of his left-hand fingers – and smoked. His gaze was unwandering.

To Tim's right, Nick was splayed face-down across the discomposed bedclothes, his head straying onto a corner of Belle's cushion pile. His hat had fallen off and his hooded top was hunched like a carapace some way up the back of his neck. Belle's legs were arched over him – floaty-trousered – her toes touching and her eyes steady on the burning tip of Tim's joint.

Fay watched the passing hedgerows and thought about Dartmoor, where she'd lived before her parents moved to Bristol. They'd had a farm at the head of a valley, a square of buildings with a yard in the middle. When you drove up the track from the nearest road you could hardly see the house at all; just the barns with their thick stone walls, slitted in the hay-lofts, impenetrable-looking as a castle.

Fay would go out on the moor at night, climb the tor behind the house and follow a path till the hill levelled off and the lights from the house disappeared. There was a rock up there: a huge, glacial thing with a niche in its side that she'd always fitted in perfectly. She'd sit there for two hours sometimes, wrapped in an enormous coat, buffeted by the wind or rain or snow, insensible to anything else.

– When did you get this ambulance, then? she said, turning to Pete.

– Oh… said Pete. Five, six years ago, maybe? I don't know. I'd been on this bender. I think I was at the Electrick Temple or Return to the Source or somewhere like that – to begin with anyway. It was when them places were still kind of new. Do you know what I mean? Basically, I woke up one day naked on the floor of some flat I'd never seen before, and I'd got this bloody sun tattooed on my stomach!

– The war scar, said Fay.

– The war scar, said Pete. I mean, it was pretty rough when I found it. I had to get it tidied up and finished off and that… Like, to begin with, I thought it was a joke or something, except for it wouldn't come off. I'm not even sure that I didn't go and get it done myself.

– Urla troia! moaned Paolo.

– Anyway, so I was wandering round Leeds with my brain deep-fried. No girlfriend, no flat, no job, no fucking car… I reckoned I had to possess something, do you know what I mean? Basically, anyway, I wound up at this police auction thing and got the ambulance for fifty quid I was supposed to have been saving. There's always something wrong with it – the brakes or the carb – but it's not bad for fifty quid.

– I once stopped breathing and woke up in an ambulance, said Fay. There was a drip in my arm and stuff, and one of those things they stick in your nose. No tattoo, though.

– What was that, then? said Pete. He glanced at her, then double-declutched as the lane began to incline. Booze?

– A mixture, said Fay. Various things, all jumbled up together. I didn't even drink for six months after that. I mean, I still hardly do anything now. It was just a couple of years when I kind of went ballistic.

Pete was looking quizzically at the meters behind the

steering-wheel.

– I never knew about that, he said eventually. Funny, isn't it? I mean, all the time we've spent as a group and nobody really knows a thing about what anybody else was like before. It's like, the way you are on the first day of the first year, that's the way you stay. Except for the odd story when something groovy happened, someone went travelling or something, that's it. I'd never even thought about it. I just assumed you'd always been straight.

– Oh, I have been, for ages. But... I mean, I did want to know what all the fuss was about. You know? It's like, you went to Castlemorton, didn't you? That massive Spiral Tribe rave. I mean, things like that are a big deal when you're at school and everything. I'm not saying that's why you went, but... when I was seventeen or eighteen or whatever, I was really needing something. You know? I felt empty, like there was this bloody great hollow inside me. So I started doing drugs and going to parties and stuff; but pills and acid and what have you, they're not about closing you down. Do you know what I mean?

– It's funny, said Pete, a moment or two later, I couldn't hardly remember Castlemorton the Monday morning after it happened. It kind of hardens, though. It becomes more solid, more... important. You should have seen the papers that week, though! Screaming about anarchy and what have you. I tell you, my skin was bristling the whole way down my body. Every bit of it! I mean, I know what you're saying, and you're probably right. That sort of thing was good cred, but... It was just like – us and them – and we were alive even if them fuckers weren't! I believed in it, you know? Basically... I still do.

93

With a roar, the ambulance topped the hill and began meandering – idling – down the other side, the road ahead of it silvery in the moonlight. Over to the right, exposed-looking lines of street-lights were woven together as if for mutual security. Slowly the moon swung away leftwards. Pavements pushed back the hedges. Fractionally different houses and regular orange light-bulbs rolled in from either side.

Having left Dartmoor, Fay had never quite felt the same about it again. She loved it, of course, but returning was just that. The immense spaces weren't the same without the farm to go back to; the kitchen and its hexagonal tiles, the dog sprawled under the table. She'd started to drive back down there on her own when she was old enough, parking just down the track from the farmyard and climbing the tor till she got to her rock. The niche was too small for her now, obviously, but she'd sit on another part, pressing her knees to her chest, closing her eyes, feeling the wind and hoping to be absorbed by it – even for a moment.

That probably was why she'd had the dangerous phase, Fay reflected. Dartmoor, then four years' perplexity, then wastedness because she just hadn't felt like herself any more. None of them had, if she were honest about it. Her parents had drunk gin, and watched television, and ceased talking to one another; and in the end she'd only really recognised her dad in the evenings, for about half an hour before he fell asleep. Fay had just felt like she was withering, becoming someone else's idea of herself, like her real self had dumped her and pissed off across Dartmoor, whooping and cheering because it didn't have to worry about keeping warm or eating or any of that physical palaver any more.

94

Tim hadn't so much as twitched in the last twenty minutes, so Belle crawled across the bedclothes and pulled the half-smoked joint from his fingers. Tim's eyes opened a little, but he said nothing.

– I am not just a pretty face! said Paolo drowsily.

He stretched – rolled his shoulders – then reached into a trouser pocket, removing his phone and wallet and stowing them in the glove compartment. Once he was comfortable, he closed his eyes and reconjured up Fifi.

The ambulance was coming to a gradient, beginning to struggle, brown-leaved hedges tight around the mirrors. In front, a badger trundled unconcernedly across the lane, locating its path through the undergrowth and scaling the bank.

– Bollocks! muttered Pete.

He began to grow rigid over the wheel, willing the ambulance onwards; then he frowned and, abruptly, swung the wheel left, stopping the engine in an open gateway. The headlights were on a dozen or so large, round bales that someone had arranged into the shape of a steam train.

– Shit, shit, shit! he said, jumping down from the step and hurrying round to the front.

A moment later he was back at the door.

– Belle! he said urgently. Pass us a drape out, would you?

– What? said Belle, half-asleep. What's going on?

– Just pass us a drape, Belle. Please.

An arm extended from the back into the cab, an ornately patterned bedspread hanging from its hand. Pete grabbed it and wrapped it hastily around his own arm, heading back to the bonnet and releasing the catch in a smoke signal of steam, smothering the window in condensation.

95

– Madonna! said Paolo, waking suddenly. Fuck! Pete, what's happened?

– We've got a flat tyre, said Pete sourly. What do you think?

– No! exclaimed Paolo.

– No, what? said Pete, retying the drape around his arm.

– No! said Paolo again. A flat tyre? It's not possible!

– Paolo, you are a halfwit. Pete gripped the radiator cap and twisted it.

A plume of steam exploded into the air. Fay climbed down from the passenger side, watching as it slackened.

– The bloody temperature gauge's bust, said Pete.

– Oh shit, said Fay. Oh well. It'll cool down in a bit. Wicked train, don't you think?

She walked over to inspect it, her face white in the glare of the headlights, her hair in a ponytail, doing the zip on her fleece up to the neck.

The train had four round bales for its wheels. It had three in a cylinder for its body, and for a funnel and a cab respectively it had two heaped at the near end and one at the far. Both were crowned with a thatch of grass. Connected by a piece of rope, the tender was a bale laid lengthways, with another at each end for wheels.

Pete lit a cigarette, leaning against the front of the ambulance, watching as Fay climbed in stages onto the cab and sat down. She looked out over the hedges, shoulders back, legs hanging loosely. Away down the hill, the town stood out in dots of orange. The main road was a shadow and a pair of passing lights. Small, sinuous hills lay in folds across the countryside, their crests picked out by the moon.

It was straight above the funnel – due west – close enough to the ground now to pronounce the missing sliver.

m: open sesame

Strange that the sky should elect to be blue. Strange too that it should be grey – or red, for that matter – but there was something more, something proportioning, about blueness. It put Pete in mind of painting lessons at primary school: the stratum of blue they'd all laid out along the tops of their pictures, with mothers, or houses, or dogs underneath. The memory still jarred when he thought of it, the teacher leading everyone out into the playground and asking if anyone could actually point to the blue streak they insisted on painting.

– Don't know… they'd mumbled, one after another, when asked why they did it.

It had been miserable, trooping back inside and filling everything between the earth and the ether in with a blue felt-tip.

The evening before, Pete remembered, he'd spent pressed up against the television, one skewy eye shut, trying to see what went on around the corner. Although he hadn't quite managed it, the idea had possessed him of looking at something more than house, mother and dog, through something larger than a little window. So he'd painted the earth – a blue and green splodge – with a fat blue line just above it. A really good idea, he reflected, much better than everything being blue. It was like, to see the mother, house and dog in the first place everything couldn't be smothered in blueness, right? It had to change somewhere. And his changing place had been a fat blue line in space. You'd never see that through a little window of a picture.

The teacher had sighed when she saw it, and made him do another one with the dog and the sky and everything on it like it was supposed to be. She'd kept a bit of an eye on him from then on, and once told his mother at a parents' meeting that he was, quote, Too much of an individual for his own good.

Pete was lying across the front seats of the ambulance, his head tipped back, looking at the twigs hanging upside down into the blueness, the auburn leaves, the ridge of the Black Mountain that traced the line of the windowsill. It seemed like such a long time since he'd looked at anything above the horizontal.

It was the pangs for nicotine, though, that finally made him pull himself upright. He folded the blanket he'd been wrapped in, sitting it on the seat beside him and fumbling through his pockets till he'd mustered enough tobacco for a cigarette: dry old bits that kept getting in his mouth and making him cough.

On the passenger side of the ambulance, a bank sloped towards a small, gorged stream. With a last puff, Pete threw away the cigarette and climbed inelegantly out onto the lane they were parked beside. He tied his heavy brown dreadlocks into a knot on top of his head, and went to splash water on his face. Behind him, the sun was beginning to make its way over the mountains, a shadow sliding down the west face of the valley.

98   Then, as he crouched beside the water, light grazed the top of a beech tree on the opposite bank, and an oak, and another beech; and, gradually, the brown of the leaves on every side of him became reds and oranges, greens and golds.

The sky itself seemed to sparkle as Pete reclimbed the bank. There was still no sound from the back of the ambulance, so he sat on a gate across the road, looking over a field with a pair of firs in its middle and the long, level Black Mountain running past behind it.

The car approached quietly, appearing round a corner to Pete's right, gleaming white in the sunshine. It was an Austin Maestro, not in the best of states, its police stickers starting to peel and rust in patches on the wheel arches. It drove slowly past Pete, then stopped, and reversed.

– Alright? asked the officer, leaning an arm on the sill and squinting against the sunlight.

He was sinewy-looking man, improbable in his uniform, with bushy sideburns and shaggy black hair. His eyes ran over Pete's dreadlocks, his piercings and drooping clothes. He looked more curious than suspicious.

– Fine, said Pete nervously, revolving on the gate to face him. I, um… It was getting late, so, you know, I thought I'd better stop for a rest.

– Been here the night, have you? asked the officer.

– Just a few hours, officer, said Pete.

– Well, I just thought I'd check you'd not broken down or anything.

– Oh no, said Pete hastily. No, everything's fine.

The man raised a hand to shade his eyes.

– What is it, then? Three-litre?

– Er, yeah… Three-litre, diesel. It's a Tranny, basically.

– Used to have one myself, reflected the policeman. No end of trouble it was. No bloody end. Just like this thing, as it goes.

He tapped the Maestro.

– A bit of a pair… said Pete.

The policeman chuckled.

– Damn right they are! Bloody junk! A Tranny to save people's lives, and a Maestro to chase criminals! What in God's name were they thinking? He chuckled again. You come a long way, then?

– London, said Pete, unthinkingly.

99

– London, echoed the officer. I went down there one time. Before I was a copper…

He paused as if waiting for Pete to press him on the subject, but resumed anyway when he didn't.

– Not my sort of place, if you don't mind me saying. No offence, like. Bloody noisy it was. I was in… round the middle, it was. Can't remember too much about it, tell you the truth. Lot of houses and pubs. By Christ, we got pissed!

– Were you down there long? asked Pete.

– Oh, just for the game. Long enough, though, I don't mind telling you… Where you headed?

– To be honest, said Pete, I'm not really sure where we are right now, but I'm supposed to be in a place called… Llyswen? You know it? Near Hay-on-Wye.

– Ah, Llyswen, said the policeman. He frowned and glanced along the valley. Well, you're on the right road. Just keep going straight, over the Gospel Pass. Take the first left once you're out on the flat there. You can't miss it… I'm off to Hay now, as it goes. 'Fact, I'd better be getting along.

– Thanks, said Pete.

– That's alright. Cheerio, then.

He nodded.

– Cheerio, said Pete.

The Maestro rolled slowly off along the lane, skirting the perimeter of the field and becoming lost among trees where the road curled left.

Out on the road, Belle was gazing at the mountains, her arms out to either side of her. Now that the sun was a little higher, the reddish-brown bracken on the mountains had started to glow. Even the rowans and the hawthorn trees were shining. Pete was perched on the gate he'd been perched on all morning, rooting through his pockets for more tobacco. A little way down the lane Fay was sitting cross-legged on the verge, scribbling in bursts in a notebook.

Belle wanted a cigarette. She really wished that she could just stand there with her arms out – warm air on her skin, a germ of elation in her stomach – and find it all enough. But the idea of a cigarette kept worming its way back into her head, promising it would make the germ consummate. It was like, when she felt happy she always wanted to feel *happy*: pilled-up happy. If a feeling wasn't perfect, it was never quite there. That was why she would sometimes make out that things were wonderful, when really they weren't that great, or go on about psychic or emotional bonds with people, which, in truth, weren't as striking as she did really want them to be. She was always trying to wish things into existence. It worried her sometimes.

– This is it, said Pete, gesturing with a second, miserable roll-up. It was all I could scavenge from the cab, my pockets, everywhere... Maybe Tim's got some. I don't know. I don't suppose Paolo has.

Belle walked round to the back of the ambulance, pressing the rubber button and swinging one of the doors open. Inside it smelt of old smoke and sweat. She wrinkled her nose and assessed the mess. She'd really slept in here?

– Tim! she said loudly. Hey, Tim!

Tim was crumpled in a corner, like he'd fallen there from somewhere high up.

– Euggh? he managed.

– Tim! Belle repeated. I need a cigarette!

– I was, Tim moaned, after a pause, visited!

– What? said Belle.

– Finished, Tim corrected himself.

Belle did a breathing exercise she'd learnt in India in her gap year: sucking in air through her nose, holding it, saying

101

Mahatma Gandhi in her head, and breathing out through her mouth. She kept up the exercise until she felt less irritable; then she returned to the others.

– We have got to get some cigarettes, she said.

A sign saying Llanthony appeared as the ambulance turned the corner at the end of the field. There was a yard on the left, a couple of farmhouses gathered round it and an oak tree in a radius of leaves in the middle. A couple of dogs were busying themselves in corners.

Behind the yard fields ran up into pine woods. Farms were sheltering in hollows, their boundaries blurring with the desolate common land where sheep were specks in the bracken and streams like vein mouldings cut their way among rocky outcrops.

– A pub! said Nick excitedly, leaning in from the back and pointing. Oh, a pub! Thankyou God!

– It's nine in the morning, said Pete soberly.

– Yeah, but... Jesus, Pete! A pub!

They drew up outside one of the Bull's oak-framed windows, Nick and Belle peering against the sunlight to try and work out if anyone was inside.

– Well, said Belle. I'm going in.

102   She swung the passenger door open and jumped down onto cobble stones, steadying herself and breathing – Mahatma Gandhi – a couple of times before approaching the heavy, tar-black door.

The room was dark and it took a moment for Belle to distinguish what was in there. Then she saw flagstones, vertical pine-panelling, a billiard table and a stone ash-filled fireplace. There were a lot of what seemed to be redundant organ stools scattered around tables peeling veneer. Dried flowers hung from the beams. The walls were covered with precise watercolours of horses.

Belle looked at the watercolours and found them entrancing. They reminded her of when she used to ride herself. There was a bay, startled in a beam of sunlight beside the window, lissom, with a star on its nose just like Stella had. She really had to go and see her again sometime.

– Oh, hi! she said suddenly.

A man in a red rugby shirt was sitting on a stool at the far end of the bar. He was staring at her, a pint of bitter in his left hand.

– Alright? he said, clearing his throat.

– I'm very well, said Belle, primly.

She smiled – thick pink lips, even teeth – then became aware that the man was inspecting her chest.

– I was, er, wondering if there might be any cigarettes for sale here, she said, embarrassed, trying to stifle her middle-class accent. I'm quite badly in need of one.

– You are, agreed the man.

Belle looked confused.

– Here, he said, changing tack. He picked up a packet of Rothman's from the bar and removed two.

– Oh... Thankyou! said Belle. I... She dithered a second then took one, leaning forward as the man lit it for her, ignoring the fact he was peering down her cleavage. Ohh! she said, exhaling. 103

Belle felt a slight headrush, then much better disposed to the world around her. She rather liked this little pub, if not so much its occupant. It had an authentic quality to it. She wondered vaguely how much it might cost.

– That was very kind, she told the man, who for some reason was rolling his shoulders like an athlete. I wonder, though. I have some friends outside who would like to buy some. Do you think...?

She smiled attractively.

– Joelene! called the man over the bar. Joelene?

– What?! shouted a voice.

– You open for cigarettes?

There was a sound of footsteps, and a round-eyed young woman in a tight, extra-large T-shirt appeared. A small boy with a scheming look about him flitted in after her. He peered at Belle around the bar, then rolled back his eyes and stuck two fingers up his nose.

– There's a machine behind the door, said the woman, gauging the situation. You help yourself.

– Thankyou very much, said Belle, smiling again and trying not to look too beautiful.

There was common land in every direction, the ridges of the Bluff and the Twmpa smaller now and the engine returning to a rumble as the road flattened out. A cattle grid purred beneath the wheels. On the far side of the valley a final farm was clinging to its fields, a great, stirrup-shaped pine plantation stretching down a cirque behind it.

There were screes, gorse bushes, weather-torn hawthorns, the gnarled banks of tiny brooks. There were footpaths resembling cartoon lightning strikes. The tails and manes of fat mountain ponies reached almost to the ground. Then the last piece of stream vanished up its spring. The mountains met in a V of seamless blue.

Pete stopped the ambulance just beyond the col, pulling into a wheel-eroded layby with a burnt-out Escort upside down on the slope below. No-one, it seemed, had been expecting the mountains to fall away so rapidly. They climbed from their various doors in silence – a couple lighting cigarettes, wonderingly – and stood in a line on the lip.

– It's different to Portmeirion, observed Belle, garnering her Welsh experience.

The skies were not in fact perfectly clear. Beyond the flood plain spread below them, beyond the bleak, lesser echo of mountains on the valley's other side, above the endless waves of hills, there was the odd wisp of whiteness: uncertain, like a smear on the lens of an optical instrument.

It was the colours that were the most striking, or perhaps the curling sheerness of the Twmpa, or the emergence of the Wye from its Welsh confinement to wander shimmering across the sudden plains of Herefordshire.

The slopes below were green – evolving from moss to emerald with their plane to the sun – ruddy brown where the bracken was thick, tawny where a decrepit baler had left stubble and damp bales. There were greys and silvers in the river; chocolate browns in the valley; reds in the wooded gorges; unfolding blues in the sky; fiery unknowableness in the sun.

Fay, for her part, thought about hedges, about enclosing things. She imagined the forested wilderness that had once covered the landscape; the people cutting piece after piece of land from it, making the unknown known, so each space acquired a sense and identity in relation to every other – like language, a structure that gave itself meaning. Looking closer, she could even see where there had once been other hedges lacing the expanse of the flood plain, where there were now only shadows.

Tim put a lighter to the joint he'd been rolling, and climbed back into the ambulance.

105

n: version

The first thing Angus saw when he opened his eyes was Grigori Efimovich Rasputin, notorious Siberian debauchee, self-proclaimed miracle worker and pernicious influence behind the Imperial Russian throne. He was looking well: the bedraggled hair less greasy than it often was and his facial expression a fitting combination of piety, near-mechanical sexual potency and a desire to get hammered immediately on vodka. So far as they could, his eyes locked onto him. He was swimming. Not paddling in the manner he may once or twice have tried before his death in the River Neva, but sort of pulsating with the pain in his temples.

Angus squeezed his eyes closed and tried to move his head enough to be confronted by something other than his own drunkenness when he opened them again.

With the vodka bottle in the corner of his vision, he was staring across the dust, mouse droppings and tattered carpet of the kitchen floor. For a moment he remained disoriented, then, in a surge, he remembered himself and the unwelcome prospect of another day. The Rasputin was practically finished. Filthy stuff it might have been, but it remained the best thing going for this horrible little cottage and now there was almost nothing between him and the emergency bottle of Vladivar.

He was lying on the rug in front of the cold iron woodburner, his head on the pair of moccasins, suffering. Even if he did prove able to get himself upright it would be a good half-hour before any hope of a cup of tea. Without milk. So for some minutes he remained where he was, frozen by the cold.

Across the room there was a noise. He became aware of it slowly: a kind of rustling scrunching. It seemed to be coming from the shelves at the end of the partition wall. Pressing a hand against a freezing flagstone, he levered himself into a sitting position, waiting a second while the room caught up with him and edged into some kind of focus, squinting in its direction.

The mouse was sitting in the fruit bowl like an old man in his particular chair in a pub. Its back legs were spread for balance and its front legs pinned securely to a peach: the only fresh piece of food left in the cottage. Now and then it seized a chunk between its teeth, enlarging the hole it had made already and chewing sensuously. It had the eyes of an errant pet.

Angus pulled himself to his feet, staring at it, steadying himself against the table. He'd hear the mice frequently – squabbling in the woodstack – and occasionally he'd see one, scurrying across the floor, but this was something altogether different.

He might not have been there at all.

– Fucking gall! he shouted.

He waved his arms, which hastened the mouse's munching but nothing more. So he picked up the bowl and shook it; at which the mouse chewed twice, swallowed, then leapt the five and a half feet to the flagstones and disappeared into the utility room.

Angus threw open the door and hurled the bowl as far as he could into the adjacent field. Which turned out not to be very far.

As usual the squirrels piled from their hole at the end of the roofspace, scrambling down the climbing rose and rushing off into the undergrowth.

107

Angus sank back onto the rug he'd woken up on, wrapping the blanket round his shoulders, shaken by the sunlight, closing his eyes. The burning in his head was swollen like an infection. Already the story was scratching to get out of him.

– Would that I had seven lives to give for my country!

The words startled me, appearing unannounced. Reaching to my right, I adjusted the volume of the radio equipment, listening intently to my headphones; but all I could hear were the roar and the vibrations of the aircraft. The other Zeroes were flickering before me, ghostly above the shadowed mass of Okinawa.

Perhaps, after all, I had uttered them myself.

– Would that I had seven lives to give for my country!

They were the words of the samurai Masashige Kusuneki, who in 1336 took his life on the banks of the Minato River, the forces of Takauji consuming his own and the Emperor Go-Daigo exposed beyond hope in the capital behind him. Six centuries of significance, dispelled in a mere ten days. How strange that they should reappear now, when they could finally be of no benefit.

Yet suddenly there was the hiss of static in the headphones, and the catch of troubled breathing. For a second or two they continued; then, with a powerful intake of breath, the Vice-Admiral began to speak:

– I alone, he declared, am to blame for our failure to defend the homeland and destroy the arrogant enemy…

His face emerged slowly in my mind: tears in streams on his noble, rounded cheeks, the hachimaki tight around his forehead, the precise movements of his mouth like a mirror to the devotion of his faith. He was weeping for all who had died, for the future in which he had believed, for the impossibility of the present, for his terrible, incurrent shame: for, in fact, everything but his own approaching death. Then I could see even the moon reflected in the streams' bead-like heads, and the intensity of the image was such that I flinched and, in that second, lost it.

– I am going to make an attack at Okinawa, the Vice-Admiral continued, where my men have fallen like cherry blossoms. There I will crash into and destroy the conceited enemy in the true spirit of Bushido, with firm conviction and faith in the eternity of Imperial Japan.

The measured flow of the words correlated with the pulse of the propeller blades. It was as if I were looking down, soaring over the mouths of successive, bottomless pipes: each with its own unblinkered view of the universe. And, through these, I began to understand some aspect of the questions that were plaguing me. If nothing else, that the Vice-Admiral had despatched men to their deaths, certain in the knowledge that the Empire could never win this war.

– I trust that the members of all units under my command will understand my motives…

And now the war was to resume, with Tokyo burnt and Nagasaki and Hiroshima razed ineffably behind us.

– …and will strive for the reconstruction of our great homeland that it may strike forever. Tenno haika. Banzai!

There were sounds outside – voices. They'd started a couple of sentences back. Angus dropped his pen and listened. A number of people were somewhere on the other side of the stream, emitting the odd shriek and yell. Conceivably, they were something to do with Mrs Lloyd, although it didn't seem especially likely. They were probably just ramblers. Lost urbanites.

Angus rose and went over to the fire to restoke it with waterlogged bits of wood, tugging on the wire attached to the handle and poking at the embers to see if they might be persuaded to burn. A flame or two appeared obligingly towards the back, so he sacrificed a piece of kindling and erected a tepee of branches around it.

The voices were getting louder. They seemed to have crossed the stream and to be working their way along the bank from the direction of the footbridge.

– Please, he found himself muttering. Sod off up across the field or something. Don't come poking around down here.

There was a deity for this function, Angus realised. He-stroke-She would be the last before global atheism, or the apocalypse, or whatever completive event. The deity of the testing situation. The ultimately assured position.

The sun had reached that point of the day when it could find its way between the trees to the east of the house and the eaves of the roof. It shone off pieces of crockery on the sill of the normally shadowed easterly window, spattering twisted bits of light across the ceiling.

– Look! a woman shouted, close enough now for words to be discernible. Look! Isn't it sweet!

Angus felt a sort of seizure in his stomach. He took a step towards the window, then changed his mind and stood away from it to avoid detection, then changed his mind again and hurried upstairs, where he lay on the bed and prayed that the voices would recede.

They didn't. Soon they were outside the door, hushed now so he could barely make out what they were saying, even through the thinness of the window beside the bed.

The knock on the door was like his heart misfiring. Angus froze, prone. It was Mrs Lloyd. It had to be. Who else, after all, ever came down here? Mrs Lloyd, and a few of her friends.

Okay, he didn't want them there but she'd visited before and he'd survived, hadn't he? They'd only be after a cup of tea or something...

There was a second knock on the door, more forceful this time, then the sound of the squirrels bounding across the roofspace and eructing from the hole at the end. Painfully, Angus pulled himself up from the bed, treading across the sagging boards of the bedroom and entering the stairwell.

The fire was crackling wetly. For a moment he stood between the table and the last step, attempting to compose himself; then he said loudly:

– Come in!

The door swung open, revealing Mrs Lloyd. Or. Four figures, all with Mrs Lloyd's head. Angus staggered backwards, the feeling in his head like a sudden, manyfold increase in atmospheric pressure.

– Hello, Angus! said the first figure, a little uncertainly.

Mrs Lloyd began to dissolve. It was Fay. And Pete, And Tim. And... Belle!

– I... said Angus.

Paolo and Nick appeared breathlessly behind them, grinning excitedly, swarming through the doorway.

o: sheep in heaven

– So, we decided we'd come and pay you a visit! enthused Belle. Good idea, don't you think?

– Er, sure, said Angus weakly. Yeah.

Belle grinned and shuffled provocatively on his lap. She was wearing a tight pair of colourful hipsters and the same croptop she'd had on beside the river the day they moved into Burnell Road. Her left breast was brushing against his chest as she talked. It was what she'd always done to arouse him when they were going out together, honed to be just about undetectable in a social situation.

– Belle! he hissed. For fuck's sake…

– Sorry! She sealed her mouth self-reprovingly, eyes conspiring.

The number of times Angus had sat in that room, imagining Belle there, just as she was. It was all so confusing he half-thought that he'd slipped into a world of fantasy, that he had after all been consumed and was sitting at his desk, staring at the wall, his eyes spiralling in colours. How would you know, after all?

For a moment or two Angus covered his face, focusing on the people in the room and seeing if he could make them all evaporate; but Belle was quite definitely pressed against him, firm and lithe as she'd ever been. Voices continued around the room. The burning was giant, consuming everything but the smallest stirring in his desertised sex drive.

Belle reached over to the back of the chair – putting an arm around him as she did so – and, unhurriedly, retrieved her bag.

Placing it on her lap, she rifled till she found a pot of aspirins, which she opened, taking out a tablet and breaking it in half. She flushed one of the pieces down her throat with most of the remaining Rasputin, and put the other half back in the pot.

In the woodburner, the fire was roaring, prompted by the pieces of dry wood Angus had been saving for an emergency. The kettles on the hotplate were issuing a half-hearted wheezing noise which the others seemed to think, wrongly, meant they were about to get some tea.

– But, Ang, what about telly and that? Nick was saying, puzzled, puffing on a joint.

– There's no electricity…

– Well, why don't you get a battery one or something?

Belle was, tinily, beginning to shuffle again on his lap.

– I… I don't want one, he said.

Nick shook his head disbelievingly and continued to pace around the ground floor, smoking, squinting at mirrors, pictures, cobwebs and the various other attractions hung about the walls. Angus hadn't seen him since he'd shaved his head. It made him look a good deal like a tortoise.

– Well, like, we could bring that stereo down from the ambulance. You know. It'd liven the place up a bit.

Eventually Belle had to go. Angus pushed her off and hurried to the sill against the far wall, collecting a porcelain teapot and a load of miscellaneous cups which clinked as he carried them. Belle was leaning against the dresser near the partition door, her hair hanging left, her smile regarding him as a challenge. She sighed and her breasts rose against her croptop, ironing out the odd wrinkle around the armpits.

Angus looked anywhere but at her, conscious of the raggedness of his jeans and jumper, his overgrown hair, his unshaved face.

– So what the fuck's this, then? said Nick, peering at one of the pictures.

The picture was *The Broad and the Narrow Way*: a landscape bisected by a stream, with a path running uphill on either side of it. The left-hand side was province of the theatre, the public house, inferred sexual promiscuity, Sunday opening, music and other sins. It culminated, on top of a hill, in a place that looked a lot like London during the Blitz. On the right-hand side were the pious: Victorians praying fervently and shewing charity upon one another. Theirs was the Narrow Way, which – despite its narrowness – consisted mainly of lost expressions and expansive lawns. It did, however, lead to the splendid celestial city, with the Lamb of God rising out of it on Its four marvellous legs.

– It's *The Broad and the Narrow Way*, isn't it? said Angus.

– What the fuck did you put that up for?

He inhaled slowly.

– Nick, he said, I didn't decorate this place. It's just how it was when I moved in. No-one's lived here since, like, before the war or something.

Nick peered at it again.

– You can tell we're in Wales, anyhow. He laughed. Look. There's only a fucking sheep in heaven!

– That's the Lamb of God, said Angus shortly.

114

– I hope we're in for an Indian summer, said Belle, looking out through the cobwebs at the tawny field rising before Llandefalle.

– Indian summer? echoed Paolo. Che cazzo! It fucking rains in India in the summer!

– That, said Belle aloofly, is the point. Why do you think it's called an Indian summer? It's sunny after it's supposed to be.

– It's called an Indian summer, said Pete from the next room, because of Red Indians, not Indian Indians.

– Excuse me, said Belle. I have been to India…?

Pete had found his way onto the chaise longue that ran beneath a window in the other room. He'd rearranged the floral dustsheet covering it, draped his dreadlocks over the end, and was sipping at a spumy cup of tea.

– Angus, he muttered, have you got a dictionary or something?

Angus stood up, went to the desk, and took one through to him.

– So, he said, where's the others, then? Where's Katy and, er…?

Belle's lustre faded visibly.

– Infatti, Paolo exclaimed, you don't know what's happened?!

– Christ, mumbled Tim.

– God, said Paolo. Well, like… Katy got pregnant, just after you left. She had to go and have an abortion.

He glanced towards Fay.

– It was with that bloke Paul, from the Biology department. You know, the one with the red hair?… Fay hesitated, inspecting her hands a moment. He dumped her when she told him. She went through it all on her own, didn't tell anyone. Then she just kind of shut down, locked herself in her room. I was really worried… In the end I phoned her mum… So, she's back at home now.

– Oh, Jesus… said Angus. Poor Katy.

– Yeah, said Paolo, and Rob pissed off to Amsterdam, and vanished…

– We got a letter from him on Monday, said Pete from the chaise longue. He's in Dunkirk Prison, doing seven months for smuggling. And on Wednesday, Paolo got the house raided by the pigs… And, by the way, it is American Indian in Indian summer. Here. Look.

115

– I believe you, said Belle, leaning on the windowsill – buttocks barely impressed – looking at the flagstones.

– I just saw a mouse! Belle announced. Down there! Scooting across the floor!

She giggled in a mixture of panic and incipient loved-upness, lifting her feet so only the toes of her trainers were on the ground, pressing her knees together nervously.

A soft, unseasonably warm breeze was wafting through the open door. The long, unscythed grass of what could loosely have been called the lawn was breathing around the doorstep, the chopping block, the ailing nettles and the elder tree. It was the first time in weeks that the cottage could even remotely have been thought idyllic.

– Bloody mice, agreed Angus. There was one in the fruit bowl when I woke up this morning. Just sitting there, looking at me, eating a peach!

Belle giggled again, her lips lingering in a rictus, her jaw starting to chew. In the corner, bowed before the makings of another joint, Tim began to laugh suddenly too, continuing for twenty or thirty seconds before falling silent again and resuming work.

– Well, um, said Angus. Come on, then. I'll give you a guided tour.

He managed to marshal Nick, Paolo, Belle and Fay into the space before the bottom of the stairs, glancing briefly back at Tim, who showed no sign of moving, and at Pete who – as cottage veteran – remained on the chaise longue, his eyes closed, smoking occasionally on a cigarette.

– Yeah, he said. Okay, well this is the stairwell. He gestured at the segmented stairs curling towards his bedroom. It dates back to, er, 1416, when Owain Glyndwr used it to… mount a dragon.

They drifted onto the upstairs floor and, over the course of two or three minutes, Angus pointed out the auxiliary banks of porcelain, the cots, trunks and mattresses of the spare room, the carpet and his huge sagging bed, where Belle perched herself proprietorially. She removed the aspirin pot from her bag, located the half-pill saved from earlier and swallowed it.

– Ooh, she murmured, these things are dynamite!

She patted the piece of bed beside her and looked at Angus pointedly, her eyes wide and legs swinging. As he sat down, she removed her hand from just before her mouth – she'd been about to suck her thumb – to just behind his back. Angus could hear his heart beating, something like a thin-skinned drum.

– Angus, she said proudly. I've worked out what I'm going to do!

She looked him in the eyes and the burning flared inside him. The arm tightened around his back. Belle, on his bed!

– What do you mean? he said. When?

– In my life. Her jaw echoed the words a couple of times. I'm going to run my own charity! Don't you think that'd be great?

There was an odd prickling on the back of Angus's neck.

– Er, sure, he said. Sounds like a plan… What field exactly?

– Ah, she said. I haven't quite got that far yet. But it's a really good idea? She smiled hopefully.

117

– Are we, er, um… Are we, er, going picking, then?

Tim was sitting on Angus's writing chair, a joint like a zeppelin drooping from a corner of his mouth. He blinked around the room a moment, then twitched, dislodging a quantity of ash onto his clean black jeans.

– Picking? said Angus. Er… What are we on now? He looked through the open door at the clear, pale-blue sky. October? Early October?

– Mid-October, Pete corrected, looking up from a copy of *Thee Psychick Bible* he was leafing through on the chaise longue.

– Mid-October, said Angus. Well, I mean, I'm no authority. I just work here, you know. But they ought to be up by now, shouldn't they?

– Might be some after that rain, said Pete.

– Why don't you come out here where we can see you? said Nick, his arms on the kitchen table and a cigarette between his thumb and forefinger.

– Because I'm fucking knackered, said Pete. You may not have noticed but I was driving all night, and placating pigs an hour before the rest of yous had even woke up.

– Ah yeah. Nick hesitated. He pulled on the cigarette. I'm knackered myself. Didn't sleep a wink last night...

He squared himself to argue, but no-one said anything.

– So where do we go? asked Fay, looking around the room, her eyes ending up on Angus.

– Well, he said, I don't know. Off up the hill there? Down the stream? I really don't know.

– I... began Tim. Smoke was spiralling from his nostrils. I, er, I was talking with Dave a week or two back. You know, er...?

– Yes, said Nick.

Tim blinked a couple of times, and frowned.

– Nah, he droned eventually. It was, ah, no, yeah, right, it was Three-Eyed Dave. Yeah. Anyway, he was on about Hay Bluff. Said he went up there one time. That's round here somewhere, isn't it?

– We came down past it, said Fay. It's on the map.

– Well, I'm going to sleep, said Pete. Bring me a few back, yeah?

Nick was staring out of the door, his jaw hanging. At some point not much earlier in the day, thirty or so sheep had been released onto the field next door. They were picking at the patches of weeds and grass sprouting from the wheat stubble, drifting across the hillside like smoke.

He came alert abruptly.

– Oh, yeah, he declared. Yeah. Me too. There's no way I'm going anywhere. I think I'll have a snooze.

– Well, said Angus. I'm coming, I guess.

He got up from the chair, feeling like a primitive computer halfway through an extremely advanced calculation.

– You can drive, Ang, said Pete sleepily. I'm not letting any of these other bastards do it.

– Ah, said Angus.

Belle was spinning on the grass outside the door.

– You remember Richmond Park, Angus? she said blissfully, leaning towards his ear and whispering. When you bent me over and fucked me against that tree? God, I thought I was going to burst.

She ran a lingering hand down the back of his leg.

The incident reappeared promptly in Angus's mind. Tearing off her knickers, a hand between her legs, and – whoomph! – he was buried in her, pressing against those smooth, firm buttocks, kissing her over her shoulder. They'd been sensitised, of course, every part of them bewitched. It was one of those Belle moments. Ecstasy itself.

Except – like the few moments of bewilderment before each day sunk in – as the memory appeared the whole three months 119 of misery piled in on top of it, so overwhelming Angus felt like he was about to pass out.

– Yeah, he managed. Well, er. Let's get on with it, then. Tim!

Tim stuffed his skunk down his sock, put his hands on the table and heaved himself upright. Fay stood too, stretched and headed for the door, undoing the zip on her fleece and shaking out her long dark hair. She had two sparks of colour, just below her cheekbones, that Angus had never seen before.

– Paolo? said Angus.

Paolo was still at the kitchen table, fashioning a figure from a wine cork and three or four coloured paper clips. Light caught the bruising down the side of his face.

– Yeah?

– You coming?

– It's Saturday, he said.

– And?

Paolo looked at him.

– It's the fucking Sabbath, Angus. Have some respect, would you?

Paolo consulted his watch, then, with a sigh, rose from his chair and walked over to the corner beside the stairwell. There he turned himself to face in the approximate direction of the east, placing his feet together and both hands over his heart while adopting what might have been a reverent attitude.

– Mincha, he explained; then he bowed slightly and began mumbling to himself, presumably in Hebrew.

p: long, thin strips
of woodland

Paolo was standing outside the cottage door, his hands in the back pockets of his mud-streaked flares and his hair in an overgrown Afro. Beside him, Nick was sitting on the chopping block, smoking anxiously. His shoulders were hunched. Every now and then he drummed his feet on the compacted earth and wood chippings around him. Both he and Paolo were listening.

Most of the things they heard were not especially useful. The sucking of the stream. The shouts of ewes at the top of the next-door field. The splutter of a distant tractor. The rush of the breeze overhead. Inside the cottage itself, there was only the odd grunt as Pete shifted on the chaise longue: his arms thrown outwards and his dreadlocks fanned Struwwelpeter-like above his head.

– He's asleep, said Paolo eventually. Let's go.

Nick took a final pull on the cigarette and flicked it away into the grass. He put his hands in the pockets of his hooded top and got to his feet, blinking stonedly. For a moment Paolo trained his ears again; then he turned and led the way down the slippery footpath towards the bridge.

– We'll have to be quick about this, he said, glancing back to check Nick was following him. I'll get the shit from the hedge, you keep a look out? Alright?

– Paolo... said Nick. Look. Man, what the fuck are we going to do?!

Paolo climbed the stile at the far end of the bridge, setting off up the bank, weaving between the trees.

– I mean, said Nick. I mean, who are we going to sell the acid to? Huh? Man, we've got the pigs after us. Yeah? Steve fucking Fisk! I mean, what the fuck are we going to do?!

The ground was beginning to level off slightly, the other side of the valley emerging from the grass in front of them. There was a quarry-scarred hillback, then hawthorns and rusty bracken, sheep-spotted fields and the creosoted barns around Pentwyn. To their left, a hedge ran straight towards the gate into the farmyard. A chestnut horse was eyeing them from the middle of the field, munching on a mouthful of grass.

– Nick, said Paolo. He slowed and waited for him, breathing haltingly. Listen to me, yeah? We're in the middle of fucking rural Wales. Okay? Nobody knows where we are. Chill out, for fuck's sake! He pushed a hand through his hair. All we've got to do is get the purification finished, then we'll have something to bargain with. Nick, that shit is worth a fortune. I mean, a fucking fortune! Believe me, Steve is going to want it.

The horse had finished eating and was starting down the field towards them, its hooves splashing mud as it crossed the long drainage delta from the yard. Nick watched it nervously, and shuffled onto Paolo's hedge side.

122   – Yeah. He faltered a moment. But, I mean, man, what about the pigs? What if..?

– Nick! Paolo interrupted. Look at this place! Do you see any pigs here? No. Right. Neither do I. You're just getting paranoid, man, I swear...

Nick said nothing, staring at the ground in front of them. Paolo turned his thoughts deliberately to Florence, the Piazza della Signoria: the great tawny block of the Palazzo Vecchio, the burning sunlight and the delicate awnings of the cafés. He could remember every moment of it. Fifi had been sitting on a stone bench, reading a magazine. She'd looked up and seen him, and not looked back down.

The farmhouse at Pentwyn came from the quarries on the hill behind it. Its yard ran sideways, a weatherboarded barn at either end and another along the bottom. Outside the front door, a largely collie mongrel was dozing on a step, a litter of puppies and functionally cut lawns to either side of it. It raised an eyelid as Nick and Paolo scurried towards the track – glancing around them guiltily – then yawned.

The track's tarmac was pitted with a mohican of grass running down its middle. The hedges beside it were thick and balding, seven feet or so high. They'd stashed everything beneath the one on the right – just outside the farm gate – the place marked hurriedly by a wedge kicked in the verge.

– Alright, said Nick. He ran his tongue round his mouth, glancing up and down the track. Let's go.

Paolo bent down and reached into a pile of mouldering leaves, producing the sports bag and the metal case immediately and handing them to Nick. He tied his hair back and pushed his head under the lowest branches, reaching for the cool-box.

There were the remains of stakes inside the hedge, although you'd never have noticed them if you weren't implanted in it. There were traces too of the layers from the hedge's last pleaching, and of etherings between the tops of the stakes. A nest was mouthing a neat o off the end of Paolo's nose – so much in keeping with the whole that it might have been the hedge-layer's signature.

– Shit! said Nick suddenly. Paolo, get out! There's someone coming!

Paolo extracted himself hurriedly.

The tines of a tractor were visible above the hedge a hundred yards away. It was thundering down the track towards them, clattering on the potholes. Paolo turned and ran back into the yard, vaulting a few stray puppies and swinging himself and the cool-box onto a dryish patch of grass on the other side of the gate. As Nick was passing him the case and the sports bag, an ageing Massey Ferguson roared into the yard, its brakes screeching.

– Pups! Pups! Pups! said the driver, flipping off the throttle lever and tying up the handbrake with baler twine.

He'd gathered up two of the puppies – a tall, weather-beaten, grey-haired man in a blue boiler suit – before he noticed Nick and Paolo.

– Hello? he said, nodding thanks as Nick collected an escaping puppy. Don't tell me that Angus fellow's actually got some friends?

– Er… One or two, said Nick, following the man into the barn beside the yard gate and depositing the puppy on a drift of hay.

– Well! said the man. He never invited you, though?

– No, said Nick. No, we just turned up.

– Ah! The man grinned. That's more like it… Grumpy bugger. See if you can't cheer him up a bit, eh?

– Well, we'll have a go.

– That's something anyway! Mary'll be pleased to bits. She goes down there every fortnight or something, check he's not drowned in the Elsan… I'm Philip Lloyd, by the way. I'm the bloke lets him stay there.

He held out a calloused, muddy hand, looked at it, wiped it cursorily on his overalls and held it out again.

– I'm Nick, said Nick, shaking it nervously. Nick Carshaw.

– Pop star, are you? said Philip Lloyd.

– Er, no, said Nick.

– Well, good luck to you anyway. You'll probably have Mary down later on, I s'pect. Just as a word of warning. She'll be wanting to get a look at you all.

– Jesus, that was close! said Paolo, picking bits of foliage out of his hair, retrieving the case and sports bag from behind a nearby water trough.

Philip Lloyd was walking towards a door on the side of the house, the dog barking and wagging simultaneously beside him.

– We have got to get this sorted out, said Nick. I'm sick to fucking death of it!

He watched the horse on the other side of the field for a moment; then he picked up the cool-box and headed quickly back downhill.

If he ever did get the money, Paolo decided, he would buy himself a Ducati. A flame-red Hyper Sport 996SPS. He'd go back down to Italy and ask around the modelling agencies for Fifi, then he'd take her away, to Greece perhaps. They could find a beach somewhere, chill, swim, make love...

– Fucking mud! Nick was complaining. No wonder I've never been to Wales before. It's shit, that's why! Tell you what, I should never have left Clapton!

He was slithering as he walked, coming over the lip where the ground dropped towards the stream, the outline of the cottage discernible through the thinning leaves of trees on the opposite bank, smoke slanting from the chimney.

His feet slid from underneath him suddenly. He landed on his coccyx, mud covering his shoes and trousers and the cool-box sitting on his lap.

– Jesus, Nick! said Paolo. What the fuck is wrong with you?! Those flasks...!

– That is the fucking limit! exclaimed Nick. That's... That's fucking it! I might just have done myself a major fucking injury and you…!

– Nick, are they alright? said Paolo seriously, bending down to investigate.

– Yes! said Nick. Yes, the flasks are alright! Am I alright? No, I am fucking not! I have got mud all over me! There's no fucking shower!

– Nick! Paolo hissed.

– I should never have listened to you and your stupid fucking scheme. Nick struggled to get back upright. You and your bloody phone call. You've ruined my Nikes! My girlfriend is going to fucking kill me…

Nick paused a second, then resumed grumbling to himself, wiping his shoes angrily on the bracken.

– Che cazzo! said Paolo, staring at him. What is wrong with me?! That's what you went back for, isn't it? That's why you went back to the house! You fucking told Sonia where we went?!

Nick looked up, opening his mouth and blinking a few times.

– What?! he said eventually. Just… What the fuck is it to you, anyway? What the fuck's it to you, even if I did?!

– Oh, porcoddue! No! said Paolo, putting the bag and the case on the ground and sinking into a squat. Frocio di merda! What the fuck have you done?! My God!

126

Nothing had changed about the cottage in the short time they'd been away. Paolo and Nick arrived on the grass outside the front door, silent as they'd been since the exchange about Sonia. Nick smoked, scraping mud off his feet. Paolo untied his hair and ran his hands through it a couple of times. In the living-room, Pete was snoring noisily.

– Alright, said Paolo finally, his voice inexpressive. We might as well get this bloody thing set up, since we can. What did you see when we were upstairs? Could we get into the attic?

Nick cleared his throat. He squashed the cigarette beneath his shoe.

– Yeah, he muttered. There's a trapdoor at the top of the stairs.

– We'd better check it out, then, said Paolo.

He kicked off his shoes and walked quietly towards the stairwell. Nick removed his trousers as well as his shoes – throwing them all in a heap against the door to the utility room – and crossing the kitchen in a pair of polka-dot boxer shorts, leaving a trail of footprints across the flagstones.

Just outside the upstairs mouth of the stairwell there was a square hole in the white plaster ceiling, an ornate black picture frame surrounding it and a piece of chipboard blocking it off. The hole was little larger than a record sleeve. Paolo eyed it dubiously.

– I'd never get through there, he said. You're going to have to do it.

He went through to the spare bedroom and collected a large, heavy naval trunk, standing it on one end. Then he removed the papers and candlesticks from the stool beside the bed – pouring them onto the bedspread – and stood it on top.

Nick, in a slightly less dirty pair of jeans, scaled the construction carefully. Once he'd got on the stool he was able to push the chipboard to one side and poke his head through the hole.

There was light – coming in beams through the cracks between the tiles, holes beneath the eaves and around the chimney – but it was a few seconds before Nick could see around the roofspace clearly. The space was prismatic – a smaller version of the attic in Kingston – that much was

127

obvious. It had no insulation or floorboards, just widely spaced joists that the plasterboards below were tacked to. As his eyes adjusted, Nick became aware of three or four old planks in a square near the eaves which someone had presumably once used to help in repairing the roof. He also made out what seemed to be a number of large piles of leaves and twigs towards the far end, above the spare bedroom.

– I think we can use it, said Nick with some conviction. There's planks we can sit it on and, like, if I'm careful, nothing should get any light on it.

– Alright, said Paolo. He was halfway down the stairs, keeping an eye on the door to the living-room, listening to the regular snores.

– Well, come on, then! said Nick anxiously. You going to pass them me or what?

He lifted his arms above him like a diver and managed to get his shoulders through the hole; then he gripped a joist on either side of him and slid his skinny frame into the roofspace. He reached immediately for the nearest of the planks – a knee on adjacent joists – pulling them towards him one by one and rearranging the square directly beneath the ridgepiece.

– Okay, he said, peering down through the hole. Let's have them then.

Paolo got himself onto the trunk – less agilely than Nick had – and reached down for the metal case. He held it gingerly, fiddling with the angle till Nick could get a hold on it.

They were halfway through repeating the procedure with the cool-box when Paolo realised suddenly that the snoring downstairs had stopped. There was a spate of coughing and the sound of footsteps moving between rooms. A chair was pulled back in the kitchen and the wheel of a Zippo rasped a couple of times.

– Pete! Paolo hissed. Nick… Here!

128

He thrust the sports bag up through the hole and lowered himself to the floor as quickly as he could. Already tobacco smoke was drifting from the stairwell.

Nick's face appeared in the frame on the ceiling. Paolo pointed downstairs, opening his eyes very wide, then at the trunk, then at the spare bedroom. Then he mimed Nick recovering the hole with the chipboard, and himself – two fingers for legs – walking downstairs, sitting down on a chair and smoking a joint – the same two fingers pressed to his lips.

Nick shifted his balance on the joists, inspected the distance to the floor and nodded reluctantly.

With the chipboard back in its place, the roofspace was now even darker. Nick crouched silently where he was for a moment, listening to the voices downstairs and the sound of the breeze in the leaves all around him.

– Alright, Pete? Sleep well?

– Er… not bad. A pause while he smoked. You're looking wired, Paolo. What's up?

– Oh, nothing. I'm, er… It's just nice here, in the countryside. You know?

Nick unzipped the sports bag, taking out a cubic battery and connecting it to the wires at the back of the cool-box. Almost imperceptibly it began to hum to itself and Nick moved it out of the way, sitting it with the battery on a joint between two joists. He then pulled out the frame of the light-proof tent – a spindly four-legged structure – which he erected on the square of planks and covered with its coating before pulling on the gloves and climbing inside with the case and the open sports bag.

As Nick worked his mind drifted over many things: Sonia in the morning, smiling as he put his arms round her but not yet able to open her eyes. Her hair, sandy and chaotic across the pillows. The snuffling laughing noise she made when he kissed her neck. It was only now that he was really starting to realise how much he missed her. How could he not have told her where he was going, for Christ's sake?

– Let's get outside, Paolo was suggesting, his voice rising and falling with enthusiasm. Check out the stream. There's some weed in Nick's... Infatti, I think I've got some skunk. It's such a nice day. It'd be a shame to waste it, huh?

Nick turned on the torch with the red bulb, hanging it from the frame above him and wiping down the boards with a rag. He only had details left to attend to – the last stages of purification – it was the main reason that he hadn't got round to sorting everything out while Paolo was away. He'd already made over two and a half flasks of d-LSD tartrate: nine hundred thousand trips' worth. They were in the cool-box, in solution, and frankly he was starting to get a bit fed up with kneeling in darkened attics, running through column chromatographies.

It had been quite good fun to start with. They'd faked the signature of one of the technicians in the Chemistry department and ordered the case, the chemicals and several boxes of ergotamine tartrate migraine tablets through the usual channels of the university. Amazingly, no-one seemed to have noticed. They'd started work in the laboratory about a week after everything was delivered, extracting d-lysergic acid from the migraine tablets and converting it into lysergic acid diethylamide.

The problem had been purification. In truth they hadn't really thought that they'd get that far without messing everything up, but then Paolo had arranged the deal with Steve and – once they looked into it – the procedures had turned out to be far simpler than most of the ones they were supposed to be doing anyway, for the course. Except the purification took time

– undisturbed hours with restricted light – and ultimately the attic was a far safer place to do it.

Two hundred grand, though! For a million trips that they didn't even have to fix to paper. Two hundred fucking grand! Eighty grand for him!

Nick flicked on the UV light a moment, checking the progress of the fluorescent lines in the chromatography column, following the fastest: the LSD line. He thought about tipping up at his dad's with eighty grand, casual-looking. Alright, dad? Yeah, not bad. What's in the briefcase? Eight fucking thousand tenners, that's what! Nick grinned to himself in the darkness. Less the balding smart-arse college-boy then, eh?

q: what makes a gander
meander in search of a goose?

– You see, it's an amazing coincidence, Belle was explaining, pinned to Angus's left arm. Quite extraordinary. Like synchronicity, you know? I decided about the charity thing, and the very next day I found out that my great-aunt was a director at Oxfam!

They were crossing the common beneath the nose of Hay Bluff, the ground almost brown with Liberty Caps: waves, pools and circles of them, two inches high and fiendishly hallucinogenic. Tim was stumbling around like a toddler a hundred yards behind them, dropping suddenly to his knees, picking with both hands and gibbering unintelligibly.

Even without Belle there, the scale was bewildering enough in itself. The Malverns were a crest a county away. The Beacons were notches in the sky above Powys. Llandefalle – Angus's normal benchmark of height and distance – was just one among dozens of little hills.

– Wow! he said feebly, trying to smile.

Belle's wide, wondering eyes locked onto his. Her face was radiant, faultless as ever. Angus found it impossible to look anywhere else.

– So she could give me all the advice I needed, then I could get some funding, which should be quite easy because I think Daddy knows some people who would help… Then I could run a charity! Wouldn't that be the greatest!

Angus was aware of Fay, her hair loose and shoulders bare, heading away towards the mountains; of Tim, shouting Ang! behind him. But he only seemed able to move as he was guided, automaton-like: thoughts and anguishes swarming irrelevantly around inside him.

To their right, the hill fell down through dingles, woods and slope-small fields towards the Wye valley. To their left, the twin faces of the Black Mountains receded twelve and fifteen miles from the Bluff, scarred by streams which cut across the common land, radiating outwards in their own tiny valleys. It was one of these, so far as he could tell, that Belle was aiming them for.

She wound her arm round the tangle of his left and her right arms, letting her head fall sideways onto his shoulder, lips parted, possibly in invitation.

– Well, she resumed, having nuzzled him a moment. So long as we remain in constant communion with God, everything'll be okay, huh?

She withdrew her head and looked up at him for confirmation.

– Er, said Angus. Belle, you haven't become a Christian, have you?

– Oh no! said Belle, tightening her arms and giggling. I just meant the Divine Source!

– Then who have you been talking to?

– Here in the countryside, she continued, It feels so much closer. I really must move to the countryside. Mmm! Somewhere with a lake! And perhaps an avenue… I can hardly keep going back to Clapham forever, can I?

The side of one of the tiny valleys was dropping away beneath them: grass-sided, ten or so feet deep with a small, fat, muddy stream at the bottom. Belle talked a moment more about dovecots and rose-girded archways, and they continued down the slope in silence: Belle with her curves, her eyeliner

133

and her long blonde hair; Angus with his short-sleeved shirt open halfway down his chest, his eyes blue and intent-looking.

– You know the last time we did this? she said. In Norfolk? Jumping those channels. Remember? Come on! We jump at the same time!

Angus stumbled as he landed on the other side, his legs weak like an invalid's. Belle kissed him suddenly, her tongue snaking between his lips. She bounded a few more feet up the bank then span back round to face him, the sun blinding, directly above her head so he had to cover his eyes.

– Angus! she said reginally. Make love to me! Come on! You know you have to. Here, on the ground!

She was probably smiling feverishly, munching on the sensation of munching; but all Angus could see were after-images – a storm of shapeless lights.

– Belle, he managed. Belle, you're off your face...

– Ah! she said gleefully. But I'm on the pill! Come on, let's just do it! No-one will see.

She took hold of his right hand and, lifting the left-hand side of her croptop, placed his hand on her breast, closing his fingers around her nipple and groaning with pleasure. Weakness flooded his stomach. Faint through the lights, she was reaching for his jeans.

134

He stumbled backwards, his feet slipping on the bank.

– Angus?! she said. What... What the hell are you doing?!

– What am I doing? said Angus, finding a voice from somewhere. What am I doing?! Belle, how the fuck can you ask me that? Once upon a time, you... You didn't even dump me. You just began shagging Rob whenever I went out of the house. There was an incident involving you tied down to our bed, with your arse in the air and Rob – how shall I put this?

– where the sun does not shine... I walked in on you, if you recall?

Belle looked startled. There was a lot of white in her eyes. Slowly she covered her bare breast with her right hand.

– Perhaps you don't, he said. Who knows? But you've just turned up, unannounced, three months after this sordid incident and under the impression that we're back in the glory days... Belle, just because no-one else knows about what happened doesn't mean to say that it didn't! It did! I swear to you, it very, very much did! Belle?

Belle said nothing. Her eyes had turned to her feet. Angus waited a moment.

– I loved you, he said. Really, Belle, I did. More than I can possibly describe. You were... You made me whole. You know? You made me feel complete. I would have forgiven you. I'd have appreciated it so much if you'd just apologised or something. Or just, you know, given me some little intimation that I existed in your eyes. Because I didn't have anything else... Do you know that?

Belle was standing now as she had been, on a slight hummock in the miniature hillside. She lifted her eyes hesitantly – wounded – blinking a little.

– I know about this, she said eventually. She faltered and pulled a cigarette packet from her bag, lighting one and filling her lungs a couple of times. I know about this. I know what you're doing. You're manipulating me through guilt!

– Belle, said Angus sadly. If you feel guilty, you know it's not my fault.

– Well then, she said, sliding the cloth perfunctorily back over her breast. If I've come all the way out here just to be insulted, I'll... go and talk to someone else!

135

Angus leapt from stone to stone across the stream splitting the Bluff from the Twmpa. The ground on the other side twisted sharply to the right. It was steeper, confused by bracken and gorse bushes, striated with sheep paths and a lane some way downhill.

He felt, he supposed, as you would after several particularly violent months at sea. The ground was trapped in a moment of tipping; so the glacial wave of the mountains didn't seem frozen but perpetually breaking on top of him. There were buzzards, circling on the updraught, a kite above Rhos Dirion, crows in the trees around the lane. He didn't feel like enough carrion to go round.

After ten or fifteen minutes' scrambling, he came to a bare patch of grass where he sank into a crouch, closing his eyes, waiting to start vomiting.

The after-images were still there inside his eyelids – shard-like lights and pieces of silhouette – fainter now, of course, but charged all the same with a sense of juncture. In the queasy darkness, his eyes began to follow them, radiating out from a central point and vanishing, surprising him when he realised like REM can when you're drifting uneasily into sleep. Then it struck him – suddenly – that the burning had gone.

There was nothing but a pinprick of whiteness.

His eyes blinked open. About fifty yards in front of him, a red Nissan hatchback was moving tentatively towards the ford of the stream he'd crossed earlier. Lining the lane's lower verge was a ramshackle wall with a scrawny hawthorn hedge poking above it. The hedge, it seemed, had been unmaintained for years. Like miniature Burnham Woods all four of the field's hedges were advancing across the grass, their vanguards the tattered remnants of nettles and jack-by-the-hedge.

Beyond the lowest of these boundaries the ground dropped quickly. Angus could see nothing else before the foothills: the heavy green pine plantations, the fiery browns of oak woodland, a valley cut by the stream that forded the lane, continuing on its obdurate way towards the Wye.

Sitting on a carrier bag with the rangy red bracken all round him, Angus was clueless what to do next. There were tears on his cheeks – he could feel them – sticking and drying on his erratic stubble; but he didn't really feel sad, or numb, or even empty.

They were still some way back up the hill behind him when Angus first heard the squelching of feet. They came only in moments – the spaces between bird calls or gusts in the bracken – but then they were slithering closer and louder. He wiped his eyes hurriedly on his shirt.

– Alright, Ang? Tim droned, arriving in the clearing. He sat on the ground beside him, discovered it was wet, frowned and stood back up again.

– Alright, said Angus.

– Check these out! said Tim, squatting.

He unwound the neck of a carrier bag, and revealed a mass of mushrooms of a similar size to a football. He grinned and his skin tightened.

– Wicked! he said. There's got to be thousands in here. I mean, if they're about four hundred to an ounce dried, and say we've got, like four thousand or something, yeah? Well, that's like ten ounces alone! And Dave – my mate, yeah? – he can get shrooms swapped ounce for ounce with African bush. We're talking eight, nine hundred quid just selling the weed on straight in ounces!

– Oh yeah? said Angus, a bit remotely. Well, you can have these anyway. Share a few out when we get back or something. I don't really think I'm up to them…

137

He pulled himself into a squat and handed Tim the PJ: Clothing for Men! bag he'd been sitting on. He took a Spar one from his pocket and sat on that instead.

– Cheers, said Tim, inspecting the contents. Yeah, that's cool… I've got this idea that maybe I could take a few hundred and refine the psilocybin and try to make some tablets out of it.

– Why not? said Angus.

Tim reached into a pocket of his mud-spattered black jeans and pulled out a packet of blue king-size rizlas and a couple of loose, broken menthol cigarettes. He sat on the PJ: Clothing for Men! bag himself.

– Like, he said, you've got A and E and K and that already. You could call it P or something.

– Mmm, said Angus.

– I mean, I've even been thinking of putting some of these on my Schedule for next year's Glastonbury Festival… Have you seen my Schedule? I did it before you left.

– You did it the first day after the last one.

– Yeah, but I've coloured it in now, too. I'm not sure if it might be too late to start changing it all around?

– Glastonbury's next June, said Angus.

– I suppose that should be long enough, really… Tim closed his eyes, inhaling delicately.

– You've been eating them too? said Angus.

– Just getting the first rushes.

There was a pause in which Tim stuck rizlas together and Angus looked west towards the Brecon Beacons – the peaks of Gwaun Rhudd rearing like a volcano – then back towards the Bluff, wondering where Fay had got to. The common land was empty so he turned his eyes to the rocks and screes higher up.

She was perched on a boulder, just on the Bluff side of a waterfall in the boundary stream – looking across the valley, her legs tucked up to her chest and her arms wrapped around them,

138

her hair floating on the mountains' updraught. She looked happy, he thought for some reason. It was something in her stillness.

– Tim? said Angus, turning back to look at him. Everything in Kingston's a bit fucked up now, right? So I mean, like, with Katy gone and everything, how's Fay dealing with it all? I mean, it's not really her scene anyway, is it? Is she… alright?

– Huh. Tim smiled faintly. With a small, respectful bow of his head he began to break skunk into his hand, lifting his knees to shield it from the breeze.

– Er, yeah, he said, a moment or two later. Yeah, well, like, I guess she's kind of a bit stressed, you know? Like, she's in her room a lot… Keeps washing her hands like she did last year when she used to come and stay with Katy… He started to crumble in tobacco and mixed it with the skunk in his left palm. But, like, I mean, she's probably alrighter than the rest of us. You know? I mean, to be honest, Belle isn't so great either. She never goes out. Just watches TV. He laid the rizla on the mix, held it down with his right hand and turned both hands over together. It's like, at least Fay still goes to college and that. Writes essays…

Angus looked at Tim with surprise. It was the longest speech that he'd ever heard him make, about anything other than drugs.

– So what about you, then? said Angus. How have you been?   139

– Oh, you know. Tim lit his joint and held in the smoke for a few seconds. I, er… It passes me by. I mean, I've never been big on normality anyway. Do you know what I mean?

Back on the common land, the sun had fallen some way towards the waiting horizon, casting a shadow over the east face of the Black Mountains, the line of its end running straight down the nose of the Bluff. The west face was acquiring some of the focus of the evening: each detail standing apart from its background, its colours intensifying until, in an hour or so, they would flare and die back into darkness.

Belle was lying on the grass beside the ambulance when Angus got back there, balled like a foetus.

– Belle? he said.

– Where's the keys? said Belle miserably.

– They're in my pocket, said Angus. Here, come on. You can lie down on the futon.

Belle moaned again but remained where she was, so he undid the lock on the rear doors, pressed the black button and pulled them open for her to get inside.

A beam of sunlight struck a poster on the left-hand wall: a gorgonic woman with staring eyes. The picture was bewitching. Angus wasn't exactly sure if the woman was supposed to be Medusa, but if you looked closely into the darkness tracing the poster's edge you could make out the frame of a mirror.

Like the sun regarding the moon.

– Tim? Belle pushed herself up onto her elbows. Have you got any more pills? Or… anything? Please?

She was shivering noticeably, the side of her trousers and croptop dark with damp.

– Jesus, Belle, said Angus.

140   He reached into the back of the ambulance and found an orange blanket that had once covered the sofa in the living-room in Kingston. He dropped it over her shoulders and dragged her up to her feet.

Belle staggered round to the rear doors and fell flat onto the bedclothes, her legs sticking out of the back. It was a peculiar sensation, touching her now the burning had almost vanished. She was beautiful, of course, even in the middle of a shitty comedown, but all he really felt looking at her was detached.

– Nah, said Tim, who seemed to be losing touch with time. Sorry. The only pills I've got are back at Angus's.

He wandered round to the bumper and sank onto the edge of a pillow, rooting for a lighter in his pockets and relighting the half-spliff still hanging from his mouth. When Belle smelt the smoke she began to make whimpering noises, so after a few more hits Tim passed it on to her, which seemed to calm her down.

Those bloody comedowns. Some had stayed in Angus's head, like cerebral scar tissue. Yawning normality. Sudden spaces in the stream of ecstasy. The desperation not to come down like that part of you that had always wanted your parents to guard you, to keep you from having to shoulder your own responsibility. Not like acid. No matter how good the trip was, on acid he'd always felt a bit of relief when the blinkers reasserted themselves.

Fay approached from the direction of the Twmpa, appearing on a wave of common land, following a path among gorse bushes and mountain ponies. Drawing closer, she began to come into focus: the fleece around her waist, her shoulders back and uncovered. Her hair was messy, lighter somehow than Angus had always thought of it. Her face was suffused with colour.

She gestured at the mountains when she saw him, grinning. 141

– Wazooks! she said. No wonder you live here!

– Yeah, said Angus. Well, it is a good day for it.

– All my own work, said Fay, grinning again.

She threw a slightly filled carrier bag onto the front seat of the ambulance, then noticed the shadow bisecting the Bluff.

– Shit! she said. Did you see this?

– Wicked, huh? He joined her on the driver's side. It was a bit more precise than that earlier... Kind of more polarised.

There were shadows reaching from the outcrops on the side facing north. They picked out minute stream beds in the mountains' surface, shrouding the gully between the Bluff and the Twmpa entirely.

– I like it like this, said Fay decidedly. This sort of precision.

He knew there was something wrong the moment he lifted the clutch. The ambulance groaned, creeping forward a foot or two like it was hobbled.

– Oh shit, said Fay. A bloody flat tyre.

Angus pulled on the handbrake, rubbed the back of his neck, turned off the ignition.

The sky to the west was thickening into orange, clouds materialising obligingly above the Beacons, the shadows of hills draping themselves across the valleys.

Fay climbed out of the passenger door and stood inspecting the front left tyre, which was spreading at the bottom as if it had melted. On the near edge, just above the ground, a fencing staple was poking from the remoulded tread.

– Right, said Angus, heading towards the back of the ambulance. I'd better get the stuff.

Fay bent down and inspected the wheel.

– It's fine, she reported. Pretty tidy. No rust.

Tim was sitting immediately inside on the heaped-up drape against the wall. He eyed Angus curiously a moment, then without warning started to laugh, launching himself from the rear bumper and wandering away across the grass. Belle was lying face down, wrapped in the orange blanket, breathing unevenly round her thumb.

– Belle, said Angus. Belle, we've got to get at the spare tyre. You're going to have to move.

– Can't, she mumbled.

Some way across the rolling, reddening common Tim was struck by something even funnier than the last thing and fell over. Angus climbed inside and, apologising, hoisted a side of the futon off the floor so Belle rolled towards the wall.

– Bastard, she managed, but still didn't move.

He flipped open the catch on the spare-tyre compartment and looked inside.

It was empty.

In a subsidiary compartment, the jack and all of the tools were gathered neatly, as you'd have expected from Pete; but the tyre was unquestionably not there.

– That's really... strange, said Fay, leaning in from behind him.

– I want a cigarette, said Belle faintly, pressed into the folded drape at the bottom of the wall.

– Well, can you see anything? said Angus.

– I'm squashed against the wall, said Belle.

– Okay, said Fay. So it's empty.

– Yeah, said Angus. You're right, though. It's really not like Pete to leave the spare behind.

– He must have just forgotten it in the rush, said Fay. I'm quite sure it's nowhere else in here.

Angus let the lid of the compartment fall closed, then he flattened out the futon and rolled Belle onto her back so she could breathe properly. She twitched a few times and took her thumb out of her mouth.

143

– I want a cigarette, she repeated. And some water.

– Bollocks! said Angus generally.

Fay produced a Marlboro from a pocket of the fleece round her waist, lighting it and poking it into Belle's mouth. She took a water bottle from her bag and laid it on her stomach.

– Hey! she said suddenly. I just thought of something!

She rubbed her hands together and climbed past Belle into the back, scrambling over the bedclothes, steadying herself against the gorgon and sliding feet first through the space into the cab.

– Yes! she said, a moment later.

Paolo's mobile phone was glowing as she held it up.

– Ha! He put it in the glove compartment last night. Buried it too, except – fortunately – I was watching! Know any good garages?

A whiteness was pushing itself upwards through the echoed red above the mountains. It was a becoming process. By the time the moon emerged, full, it had all but dispelled the last of the daylight.

– Parties for some of us, said Angus despondently, turning the phone back off.

– Werewolves for others, said Fay.

She leant beside him on the front of the ambulance.

r: ejection

– So why couldn't he just have put cocksucking bitch and been done with it? asked Inspector Hooey, guiding his Fiat Punto round the tight one-way curve at the end of Staines high street. I mean, female canine fellatrix? It could have meant a woman who… Well, we might have mistaken it for a code or something.

Norman Teather rubbed a hand on his overgrowing chin. A stream of pushchairs and shopping trolleys was passing in front of the headlights. On either side, people were swarming around the car park and the Elmsleigh Shopping Centre, the zebra crossing between them like the neck of an hourglass.

– Well, he said, I never even realised that the translator was just some polylingual bloke in Guildford. I mean, a system like Enfopol should have a programme for this sort of thing, not a Venezuelan student with a couple of dictionaries and seven hungry siblings back in Ciudad Bolivar… What do you think he makes of it, for Christ's sake? I mean, *Alright Dave, can you do us for a Wizard?!* How's he supposed to know what that means? Anyway, apparently he was getting a bit fed up with it all, so he set about amusing himself with a thesaurus; which is, basically, why the call took so long to come through. Norris said that he still hadn't stopped laughing about fellatrix when he grilled him the next day.

– It's a good word, Hooey conceded, releasing the handbrake and moving forward.

– It's a good word, but, let's face it, if he'd just put cocksucking bitch we might have got everything sorted out by now. Apart from anything else, we could be headed for the pub and not fucking Playtime's again.

– So what happened? asked Hooey.

– Who to? Norris?

– No. The Venezuelan.

– Oh, they gave him another chance, I think, but he's going to have to watch it.

Hooey stopped at the brake lights of a minicab, craning right for gaps in the oncoming traffic while a young woman in a small piece of material steadied herself against the minicab's right back door then leant inside to snog the driver.

To the left the houses looked squashed, like their roofs might pop off at any moment. Across the road, swans were massed against the bank of the Thames. The full moon threw a shivering reflection up off the water.

– Alright, said Hooey, eyeing the woman who was now reeling away down the towpath. I give up. What's a Wizard, then?

– A Wizard?! said Teather. Oh, come on, Hooey! Wizard: Wizard of Oz. Oz: Ounce. You should have got that one.

– Ah, Hooey murmured, preening his moustache.

– By the way, said Teather. Did you get anywhere with those students? Did you get any good leads?

– Ah! said Hooey. Er… Well, the bloke who's supposed to own the ambulance, Parsons? He's got no tax, or insurance, or anything. But… Someone broke into Burnell Road just after we left. One of the neighbours phoned up, said they saw a girl running away from it, so we sent round a car and – sure enough – someone had been in there. The tape had been cut. There was vomit on the floor and some bits of rope tied round the back of a chair. Someone had been hacking at them.

– Fuck! said Teather.

– Except the place is such a shit-hole anyway it's a bit hard to say what was there already and what wasn't.

– But I mean… said Teather. How the fuck did that happen?!

– Look, said Hooey. We don't actually know it was either of them.

– Oh, come on, Hooey! Who else would it have been?

– Alright, alright, said Hooey. If we assume it was… Well, the ropes were cut, badly – not untied – and there wasn't any blood. Also, the girl's housemates insist that they saw her at lunchtime today and she was fine, although I couldn't get them to say where she is now. We're still trying, obviously, but this is the point. If she's still alive and basically okay, she must have told him something she didn't tell us… Otherwise he'd have done something permanent to her. That's how he is.

The road ran left among semis and past the crowds around Staines train station. Commuters were crawling over the footbridge, heading for their gins and glasses of wine. On the platforms, people with pressing engagements were looking at the 5:37, which was fifty yards away with no obvious plans of moving any closer.

– So what's the story with you? asked Hooey. What's so urgent that you need me to gather you up from Staines high street?

He slowed for a junction. A breeze was stirring the twigs and the scant leaves around a streetlight in front of them. Teather was staring ahead of him, frowning.

147

– Well, it's all a bit embarrassing, he said a few seconds later. I got this call on the mobile, and it seems that something's come through on the taps, except the back-up people who were supposed to have dealt with it pressed the wrong button and forwarded the whole lot straight to Knowle Green without checking what was on it or making a copy or anything. They can't work out how to get it back again, and they're in Wantage, which doesn't exactly help. So there was a panic and

I turned out to be the only person from the department still in the Spelthorne district this weekend.

Hooey was driving faster now, both hands on the wheel, his eyes hooded purposefully. They passed a man limping on his way back from the train station; a troubled-looking woman with a cigarette adhered to a corner of her mouth and half a dozen children clustered around her.

The Punto entered Sykes Lane with a squeak from the tyres, passing between Astras and Mondeos and beneath the arching cubes of the PLAYTIME'S™ sign. The barrier was up. The cubicle was empty.

– Oh, where's the bloody security guard? said Teather, brushing a few head-shaped pieces of hair into place.

Hooey stopped the car to the right of the entrance and climbed out quickly, hanging his mobile phone on the back pocket of his chinos. He pushed on one of the three glass doors, catching it with a hand to allow Teather in behind him.

Inside there was a wall of hot, dry air. The mysterious soft toys watched them from their presentation tables.

– Alright, Norm? said the receptionist, a dark-haired woman with a prematurely lined face. I didn't expect you in tonight.

– Me neither, Janice, said Teather. You seen that security guard anywhere?

– John?

– I don't know. Whoever was supposed to have been out there.

– Gone, has he? Janice moved a copy of *Vogue* from her lap and put it on the desk in front of her.

– Yeah.

– He did say he wasn't feeling too well. Bad kebab last night, I think.

– Teather, Hooey prompted.

– Yeah, said Teather. Look, sorry about this, Janice. We're supposed to be on an emergency. I'll see you in a bit, yeah?

– Alright, Norm. Cheers.

The striplights were merciless in the blank, white corridor. They picked out the alcohol-burst blood vessels in Hooey's cheeks and the unplucked grey hairs in his moustache. They shone from Teather's pate and shadowed the pouches of his face so they seemed to swell and shrink with the passing of each light.

Teather pushed at door F, releasing further, even stuffier hotness and the smell of reconstituted vegetable soup. Two youngish men were sitting with their feet on adjacent desks at the far right-hand end of the room.

– Oh, alright Norm, said one, without moving. His face was puckered-looking and he had red hair.

– Hi Norm, said the other. What're you doing here?

Teather looked at both of them with disbelief. He ran a hand across his head again.

– For Christ's sake! he said. How long have you two been here?!

– Mmm… The red-haired man thought a moment. Noon, I think?

– Yeah, said the other.

– I ought to have guessed… He took a couple of deep breaths. Yeah. Nigel, Gareth. This is Inspector Hilary Hooey from the Drug Squad. We were at school together. Over in Kenley.

– Drug Squad, nodded Gareth, the one with the red hair. Rich pickings, hey?

Hooey looked disdainful.

– Not, he said, for all of us.

– Oh, of course, said Gareth, grinning and reaching for his soup.

149

Already Teather was flicking through file options and scrolling down lists of names, his eyes on the bank of screens covering his desk. Hooey skirted the mound of tea and soup cups huddled around the waste-paper basket, dribbles of tannin and synthesised vegetable juice soaking into the lime-green carpet. A throwing competition of some sort had obviously just been underway.

Not for all of us?! Hooey winced internally, watching the rows of figures as they unfurled over Teather's shoulder. What the hell was wrong with him? Middle age? Terminal bad temper? The white, hot windowless room was starting to feel claustrophobic. Hooey's eyes were drawn to the furthest monitor, where the words GOD IS A PIG were wandering about at random. He didn't smile.

– Alright, got it! announced Teather suddenly. It's Paolo Alkalai's phone. Can you believe they sent it into fucking Miscellaneous and Personal?

A hissing appeared from the speakers on either side of the desk – the sound fluctuating with the movements of a mobile phone – then there was a woman's voice:

– Directory enquiries. What name please?

– Er, hi. The voice was slightly uncertain, male, with a hint of East Anglia. I need a number for Thomson enquiries or something like that… Some sort of Yellow Pages-by-phone thing?

– There they are! exclaimed Teather. Got the bastards!

A detailed map of the Welsh borders had materialised on one of the central screens. Between the *n* and the *e* of a Gothic-scripted Stone Circle some way up into the Black Mountains was the flashing red light of a mobile phone.

– Er, hi. The same voice again. I need a garage in the Hay-on-Wye district that deals with breakdowns. Anything you've got.

– Oh, baby! said Teather. A breakdown!

– It was over an hour ago, Hooey pointed out.

Teather clicked on a couple of options and skipped through a succession of attempted calls to local garages; then the signal went dead.

– But, there's no-one around to help them, said Teather. So, if we got a chopper out there, we might still pick them up! It's not like theirs is a discreet vehicle after all.

Teather froze the map on the screen and jotted down the grid references of the phone signal. He passed the piece of paper to Hooey.

To his astonishment – glancing at the numbers – Hooey found himself feeling excited; like a blockage of some kind had given way inside him and a backlog of optimism had flooded his system in a moment. He hadn't really appreciated what kind of a result this might mean. Get that lot in Wales, and you'd have Steve Fisk and his crowd sewn up in days – he'd get addresses, warrants, witnesses, names – a chink. With a bit of luck, he could turn it into a scourge. In a month he could have fifty of the serious bastards sent down – murderers, thiefs – the people he'd actually joined the police force to catch in the first place. It was the sort of opportunity he'd been waiting for his entire career.

He pulled back the chair at the nearest desk, laid flat the piece of paper with the grid references on it and picked up the phone.

151

– Cathy, it's Hilary… Yeah. Look, I need a chopper… Now. There's some people broken down on a mountain in Wales. LSD manufacturers. Been after them for ages… Yeah. Mobile signal… No, look, it'll be fine but it's probably best to play it safe… Yeah, yeah. There's one in Brecon I think, for mountain rescue. Try them. One or two in Hereford. I don't know. Get the bloody SAS in on it if you have to… The OS reference is 374239. Get that? Okay. They're in a white decommissioned

Ford ambulance. Don't know the reg, but you can't miss it. Cathy, get this lot and we've got Steve... Yeah, Steve Fisk! You know what that means!... Precisely!... Yeah, I've got the mobile. Cheers... Cheers, Cathy. Bye.

Hooey sat back from his desk, his thoughts drifting towards promotion and accolades. Teather was working away on his keyboard, a pair of headphones clamped to his ears. At the other end of the room, Gareth and Nigel had reverted to cup-throwing. They were swapping stories, their voices lowered a token notch or two.

– So there we were on the stairs, said Nigel. I was supposed to have been rigging some surveillance equipment but, you know how it is, everything got mixed up and they got me in on the raid too. So we're creeping up to the door and there's voices in the flat, but nothing like anyone in there knows about us, you know. So – one, two – in goes the door!

Nigel flung down his arm in illustration.

– So we're all running inside. Freeze! Freeze! All that shit. Well, there's only two old blokes in there. Twins. Looked just the same as each other. Scared shitless, they were, and no-one else was about. There was just this smelly old dachshund scampering everywhere, and this huge old machine in the middle of the room, belching tenners into a box... Thousands of them! These blokes must have been eighty or something!

– Woh! said Gareth. He took aim and threw another cup at the bin.

– Did you see the pictures? said Hooey casually. This is the Richmond job, yeah? The Oliver brothers?

The two men looked surprised.

– You actually saw them?! said Nigel.

Hooey nodded.

This Steve Fisk business, he thought. It really could change everything...

– Yeah! said Nigel. Thing is, Gaz, we searched the place, you know. There was fake money everywhere. But this dachshund… Jesus! They had this whole porn thing going with it! You wouldn't have…!

Nigel stopped mid-sentence. On the desk in front of him, Hooey's mobile phone had exploded into a game-show theme that no-one else in the room had heard in the past ten years. Hooey answered it quickly.

– Yeah, yeah, he said. What?! You're kidding…! Well, why not…? Yeah, of course press them… Yeah, yeah. I do see. And if that fails…? There's a unit out there?! Then, shit! Get them onto it…! Yeah, yeah! Cathy, they could go any minute…! Okay. Yeah. Get them there as fast as they can. Keep me posted… Thanks.

He replaced his phone on the desk. Across the lime-green carpet, Teather was returning from the tea machine, a blue cup and its sickly-looking contents in each hand. He deposited one on the desk beside Hooey, the metal strip of the tea bag revolving slowly in its middle.

– So…? said Teather, sitting on the nearest chair and frowning enquiringly.

– So, said Hooey. The chopper in Brecon's out looking for some missing trekkers. The three in Hereford are taking school children on a tour of the local area. But apparently there's a police ground unit only ten or fifteen minutes away, and the SAS should be able to back them up.

– It ought to be enough, mused Teather, throwing his tea bag at the bin and leaving a round brown impression just above the skirting board.

Hooey threw his too, and got it in.

153

s: faith, or fated to die

Tim had sunk now into shaking. He was crouched on the ground, his eyes like craters in the remnants of the sunlight and the pale light from the moon. His lips moved in response to questions, but words or even sounds were failing to come out. Steadily his arms were tightening around his knees.

– Come on, Tim, Fay was whispering. Come on, get back into the ambulance. You'll get cold on the grass...

Angus was sitting on the rear bumper. Belle was supine on the futon behind him, a half-burnt untapped cigarette poking at an angle from her lips. Fifty yards away, Fay rolled back on her heels and looked towards them, her face tense with concern.

– Angus! she said. You couldn't have a look in the tape bag?

Angus stood up and walked round to the open passenger door, flipping on the light in the cab.

Inside it looked a lot like a bin had been emptied on the floor. Coke cans, chocolate wrappers and partly eaten sandwiches were heaped around a carrier bag spilling old cassettes – Happy Mondays, old acid-house compilations, '70s Neil Young albums, Asian Underground, everything Psychic TV ever recorded – and, some way down amongst them, a particularly choice King Tubby's tape, which he picked up and slid into the machine.

At once the air around the ambulance was filled with dub: throbbing basslines and echoed chants:

– *I went down to East Kingston, and there was peace, peace and love – love – love – love – love – love...*

– Mmmm! said Belle surprisedly from the back.

Clinging to Fay's arm, Tim dragged himself upright. He staggered across the grass towards the light and music.

– Got to have a spliff, he muttered.

He sat in his accustomed spot in the back of the ambulance and, with shivering fingers, set about assembling the ingredients.

– A result, said Fay, arriving a moment later. Well, at least he won't freeze.

– So what now? said Angus.

– I… Fay hesitated. I suppose we're just going to have to find someone to help us.

– Can you imagine a werewolf? Angus asked as he and Fay set off down the hill. I mean, can you imagine the moon doing that to someone?

The single lane of the road was shining against the dark, surrounding grass. It twined around the contours of the common – black and white in the moonlight – sinking out of sight with the start of a dingle where the left-hand side was a wall of pines.

– I think it would depend who it was, she said eventually. Not to anyone I know, but I don't think it's like, inconceivable. I… I think the moon can kind of bring something out of people.

155

She looked at him and suddenly the light caught the green in her eyes. It made Angus chuckle.

– True colours? he said.

– Yeah. That's kind of what I mean… Why did you laugh?

– Oh, it, um… Your eyes just kind of flashed green as I thought of it.

– Oh… She smiled to herself.

For a few seconds there was nothing but the sound of their feet on the tarmac, slipping unconsciously into time with one another. Angus changed his gait abruptly when he realised. When Fay spoke again, her voice had purpose to it, as if she'd been considering how to broach something.

– I hope you don't mind me asking this, but, er, it's not been too heavy, has it, having everyone turn up like this? I mean, I'd really not known quite what a… hermit you were these days.

– Erm… said Angus, and laughed nervously, scouring his brain and turning up very little. Well, I don't really know to be honest. I've not had much of a chance to think about it yet. Like, maybe I'm in a bit of a state of shock or something. Or maybe it's just not a big deal… I mean, I have to admit, it is what I've been dreading the whole time I've been out here.

– Yeah, said Fay. I'm not surprised.

– Why?

– Well, you made a decision. Right? You were living one way, and it was going to shit, so you left it behind. I mean, I have thought about it, you know. It was quite a big deal, dropping everything and heading off to Wales. Asking around pubs for somewhere to live. I mean, it is positive. I couldn't do it. But, after all that the last thing you'd want is to have the old life traipsing out here after you.

156   Angus turned his head to look at her, feeling himself frown as he did so. Fay was tying her hair back into a ponytail, the moon lying shadows beneath her cheekbones. The elegance of her face startled him.

– What? she said, returning the look.

– No, no, he said quickly. No. You've got the wrong idea. I never made… any decision. All I did was run away. I just got squashed. That's all. By Belle, and the drugs, and the… fucking purposelessness of everything.

– Okay, said Fay. But the drug thing, then. Jesus, I was there, Angus! It was clear enough. Down by the river on that day we moved in. Everyone had decided to go one way, and you'd decided to go another…

– Balls! said Angus. I didn't decide shit. It just happened! You're looking at this whole thing way too… positively.

– So what way are you looking at it?

They followed the road as it dropped, listening to the stream in the dingle in front of them. To their left, the plantation filled a third of the sky, the occasional star blinking between branches and needles.

– Okay, said Angus finally. I take your point. I didn't meant to be rude… But, I mean, Belle was everything to me. She was everything I'd ever hoped for, and… I could have been anyone, you know? She didn't give a shit about me. I was just somebody to admire her and make her feel good about herself, and… it left nothing. You know? When I found out. I had nothing left.

Fay's eyes were on the dingle.

– Well, she said, after a silence. Angus, that is kind of extreme, you know? I mean… There's more to the world than the tops of its mountains.

Fay looked a bit surprised, like the words had popped out on their own, but she carried on walking, looking straight ahead of her. 157

– Tell me something, said Angus a minute or two later.

– What?

– Just… something. Tell me, like, the greatest, maddest thing that's ever happened to you.

– Birth? said Fay.

– You're not allowed birth.

– Then… Okay. She laughed. You really want to know?

– Yeah, said Angus.

– Okay, then… One time, I was at this party in Bristol, and I met a bloke called Adrian. He was beside me on the sofa in the chill-out room. Black bloke. Cool, but kind of disaffected, you know? He had this issue going with record companies, and I was telling him about stuff I'd been thinking about, about how companies behave like organisms, how people kind of rent out their bodies to be occupied by their spirit, give them physical form or whatever… Like a sort of prostitution. I was kind of angry round then. Anyhow, I gave him this whole tirade and he got right into it. He started writing down what I was saying and adding ideas, and over about half an hour or something we kind of moulded it into a poem. I don't know why, really, it just seemed like the thing to do. Then this girl came over and started talking to him, and asked him for his autograph, and suddenly I realised that Adrian was Tricky!

– What? said Angus. Like… Tricky, Tricky?!

– Tricky! said Fay. She laughed again. Honestly! But that's not even half of it… I mean, I stuck around for a bit and I gave him my phone number but, well, basically I'd only straightened out about a month before so I still wasn't finding parties that easy. The thing is, about three days later he phoned me up and said he'd got this stuff we'd written and he wanted me to come over and do some more work on it…

158   Angus stopped and looked at her.

– No… he said. *Phase One*?!

– Yeah! said Fay. Exactly. *Phase One*. You know it, then?

– *Phase One*… *Phase One*'s wicked! It's the best thing he's done since *Maxinquaye*!

– It is pretty good, Fay admitted.

– But that's… Wait a minute. Are you saying that you…?!

– Well. Yeah, said Fay. The lyrics anyway. There's a photo of me in the cover and everything, kind of pale and wasted-looking, though I wasn't. He even asked me to write some more stuff with him, but... I was a bit of a mess round then. It all got kind of odd and intense... I've really only started trying to write again in the past few months.

– Fuck! said Angus. But I mean, Jesus, Fay! That's seriously cool! I mean... How the hell didn't I know about it?

– I don't know. Fay shrugged, smiling. I guess you didn't ask me.

To their left, a V of stars had appeared between the pine trees. At its apex was a gate with a sign tied to its middle.

– Neuadd-newydd, read Fay slowly, bending down so the moonlight shone from the lettering. Do you reckon it's a farm?

– I reckon it's worth finding out, said Angus. I mean, it can't be much later than seven o'clock. We shouldn't upset anyone too badly.

Fay untied the baler twine and swung the gate open, letting him through before doing it back up again. Ahead of them a track of compacted stone led more or less straight towards the far side of the plantation, where the dim glow of a window was discernible from the swell of a bank behind it.

As they walked, an entire cottage became apparent: its stone the same as the track's and its door and window-frames built sturdily from oak. The lawn around it was wildly overgrown, covered with an extraordinary quantity of junk.

– A skidoo! said Fay, peering at a shape inside the gateway.

Black even against the trees, there were walls of tractors and kitchen tiles, stacks of oak, beech and cedar, bicycles, the remains of a Greyhound bus, a clothes mangle, a trailer-load of gravel with weeds growing out of it and, everywhere, heap upon heap of roofing stones.

159

Fay and Angus hesitated a moment, glancing at one another, lit by the window. Angus's left collar was poking from the neck of his jumper and he pressed it back inside, then attempted to flatten his hair. He reached for the large, fish-shaped knocker, and tapped it against the door.

At once there was a racket, like hundreds of people had sprung awake in every room and were arming themselves, erecting barricades.

With a clack from the latch, the door swung open. A man stood on the doormat, inspecting them, his clothes baggy and his bald head reflecting a white globe lampshade behind him. A ring of white hair ran around the back of his head and smothered his lower face, like a halo that had fallen suddenly and become stuck.

– Hello! he said. He had a trace of a Scottish accent. How are you doing? Come in!

He turned back into a small tiled hall, opening a door on the left-hand side and waving them into a living-room.

The room they entered was entirely consistent with the yard outside it. Every inch of wall was crowded with photographs and paintings. Books were double-parked on ceiling-high bookshelves. LPs ran in a bank the entire length of the end wall. On the thick florid carpet, five unrelated armchairs were arranged in an arc around a woodburner. An ecstatic yellow labrador – apparently source of the earlier noise – was weaving among their legs, lashing at bottles and other fragile objects with its tail. In a couple of corners, Thelonious Monk was quietly playing *Hackensack*.

– Er, hi, Angus started. We're, er, sorry to bother you.

– Oh, never mind all that, said the man. Here. Have a seat. You're not in a rush, are you?

160

– Not especially, said Fay, perching on the edge of an armchair.

– Then you'll join me in a Scotch? said the man.

– I'd love to, said Fay.

– Er… Sure, said Angus, sitting. Thanks very much.

The man opened a low cabinet in the corner, exposing a collection of whiskies that Angus gawped at.

– Imperial okay?

– Oh, yes… said Angus.

The man took three heavy, cut-glass tumblers from a lower shelf, holding them up to a standard lamp to check for dust. His hands were gnarled, like a carpenter's or an old folk guitarist's.

– The wife's down in Hay, he confided. Then, with a faint edge of reserve, Either of you want… anything in it?

– Oh no, thanks, said Angus. Fay?

– Huh? said Fay. She seemed to be absorbed in a large photograph just to the left of the mantelpiece.

– You want anything in your whisky?

– Oh… I wouldn't mind a drop of soda, if you've got one.

– Soda? Sure, said the man, depositing a glass on the coffee table beside Angus and heading off into the hall.

– Not if it's any trouble…

– No trouble! he said, his voice faint already.

Fay looked around the room, then at Angus and raised her eyebrows.

– This is alright! she whispered.

Their eyes stayed meeting for a second.

– Hey, did you see these? he said, pointing at a bookshelf behind him. Look! Every Kerouac in alphabetical order! And Kesey! And back here, Kafka… Kavanagh… Keats… The entire house must be full to keep this up!

– Oh, it is, said the man, reappearing with a soda fountain and a tray of ice cubes.

He grinned and sat down. Angus glanced again at the book shelf, pulling out a hardback copy of Nat O'Hara's *Tales from Aran* and flicking through the first few pages.

– Thanks very much, said Fay politely as she received her whisky. I'm Fay, incidentally.

– I am sorry to hear that, said the man Scottishly. He then looked slightly embarrassed. Er… I'm Angus.

He held out his hand.

– I'm Angus too, said Angus, when they finished shaking.

– Another Angus! Delighted! Great race that we are! Well, here's to, er… Anguses!

The older Angus drank deeply from his whisky.

Angus closed the book and did the same.

– Tell me, he said. You wouldn't remember that line by Nat O'Hara about this stuff? Whisky, that is…

– *And purity's preserve should be/The woman and the malt whisky?*

– That's the one, said Angus.

Fay looked at him.

– Are you having a go at me? she said, running a hand along the passing labrador.

– Oh no! said Angus. Just a slight lapse of memory.

– It is a great thing, said the older Angus judiciously, that we can approach these things in our own different ways.

– Indeed it is, agreed Angus.

Fay cleared her throat, then turned back to the photograph beside the mantelpiece.

– That photograph, she said, gesturing at it. The black-and-white one. That's not… That's not Wavy Gravy in the middle there, is it?

– Yeah! said the older Angus. It is! God. How on earth did you know that?! And, believe it or not, the bloke on the left is me… The one with all the hair.

162

He patted his pate ruefully. Three men were standing in a line outside a small, thick-walled stone hut with a bare sweep of mountain cutting across the prospect behind them. They were squinting against the sun – semi-bearded, skin hardened by the elements, clothes ragged and darned repeatedly.

– Afghanistan. He sighed, taking a swig from his whisky. Truly a wild place.

– Fay, said Angus. How the hell do you know who Wavy Gravy is?

– He's not that obscure, she said. He did the announcements at Woodstock, apart from anything else…

– I know that, he said. I didn't know you did.

– You think it's likely, she said, that you'd know whether I'd know who did the announcements at bloody Woodstock?

The older Angus sat back in his chair, watching them amusedly.

The darkness of the wood lined in tight around the cottage. Angus could picture the place in winter, shielded from the furious snow on the mountains: the days of blindness, revealing themselves on sudden pale, crystal mornings. His namesake and his wife would be up here, battened down, driven – not entirely reluctantly – into the living-room's thick-curtained warmth.

Going by the photographs, his wife was something of a force. Line by line, a wide-eyed, '60s blonde had evolved into a harder, more resilient kind of beauty. You could see how they might complement one another. She seemed sharper than he did, more mercurial, more attuned to reality. You could see, too, how a different history might have found him here alone.

– So, you've got a puncture, he said, when they finally got round to the point of the visit. He cradled his refilled glass. What's the vehicle?

– It's an ambulance, said Angus. An old ambulance.

– How old?

– Um… Fourteen years?

– So… It's a modified Ford Transit, basically?

– Yeah, that's right.

– Then I may just be able to help you. Hang on a sec. I'll get my coat.

Angus followed Fay down the hall and into a russet-walled, hexagon-tiled kitchen. A Rayburn was smouldering on the left-hand side. At the far end was another sturdy oak door.

– So how's London these days? said the older Angus, reappearing from the hall with a newish fake Barbour and the labrador trailing behind him. It's been years since I last went down there.

He opened the door, picking up a torch and a socket set from an open toolbox and leading the way into a yard.

– It's… said Angus.

– It's fast, said Fay. Fast like it's hyperventilating.

– Yeah, said Angus. It's fast and, like, fragmented. The social scenes and the music scenes and the political scenes. Everyone's rushing around in different directions, you know… Unconcerted.

Skeletons of old machinery were stacked on either side of them, coloured in the twitching beam of the torch. The arm of a crane was black against the open patch of sky.

164

– Mmm, said the older Angus. I wish I could tell you I missed it.

They'd stopped beside an old Ford Transit with pictures of a huge, grinning, painted face looking out through mould on every panel. Beneath each picture were the words Willo the Clown! Just beyond it were the deep black shadows of the quarry where he made his living.

– There, he said, pointing at the well-inflated, front left tyre. You can have that if you want. It should do the job.

– Really? said Angus stupidly.

– Sure, said the older Angus.

– Well… God. Can we give you some money for it or something?

– No… No. Look. I've not seen Willo in years. I bet you anything you like this thing'll still be sitting here in thirty years' time, when its tyres have rotted into the ground. Just give us the old wheel off the ambulance.

– We really weren't expecting this! said Fay. Thankyou!

– Oh, it's no problem. He handed Fay the torch. I'll just go and get a jack. Loosen up the wheelnuts, yeah?

– There's another couple of friends of ours up there, Fay was explaining carefully. They're both a little… touched right now. In the head, if you see what I mean.

She cleared her throat.

– Oh, I shouldn't worry too much about that, said the older Angus equably. You get pretty used to mushroom casualties, living in these parts… Not to put words into your mouth, of course.

– Oh no, Fay agreed.

He coaxed the engine into a roar and pulled out of the gateway, stopping his Escort in the road while Angus swung the gate to – restraining himself from swinging on it – and retied the baler twine.

Angus climbed into the back seat quickly, hoisting the door upwards so it would stay closed. Fay looked back over the passenger seat and smiled. Behind her the headlights were colouring in the grass and shining back from the distant sheep's eyes, giving them a completely misplaced look of malevolence. The ambulance too was shining over a ridge or two of common.

165

It was then that it struck Angus that he'd been spiked. The notion appeared suddenly and, despite unmistakable ecstasy rushes in his stomach, he tensed immediately – his mind racing back through the past few hours like a low-grade search engine.

Why in God's name would anyone have spiked the Imperial? It was all he'd consumed in the past two hours. And who had any pills up here anyway? He looked again over the older Angus's bald, white-ringed head, Fay's chaotic hair, the floodlit stretch of road in front of them; and realised, to his astonishment, that he was just feeling happy.

Tim had stabilised somewhat in their absence, and was able to stand up and greet them as they climbed out of the car. He had a half-spliff in a corner of his mouth – possibly the same one, probably another.

– You want a go on this, Ang? he offered.

– Oh no, said Angus. No thanks. Better get this wheel on, you know.

Tim waved it at Fay, who made similar noises, then at the older Angus, who hummed and ha-ed then accepted, declaring through the smoke that was his first in five years.

Belle, it seemed, was asleep.

166   There was an acuteness in the air. A sense of focus and clarity. Angus carried the lorry jack from the boot of the Escort to the ambulance, aware for the first time of muscles he'd developed over the past three months: from woodcutting, he supposed, and his routine scything of the lawn.

Fay loosened the wheelnuts and Angus had the nose of the ambulance up within seconds. They swapped the wheels together, Fay hand-twisting the nuts back on while Angus ratcheted them tight.

The older Angus was chuckling as he drove away down the hill. Behind him, the moon had moved a little way westwards but it continued to light the world in black and white. The patch in the Escort's headlights was the only colour before the odd line of streetlights on the other side of the valley.

t: a man in a maestro

I can see it in your eyes.
I can hear it in your sighs.
Feel your touch and realise
The thrill is gone.

PC Andrew Price approached the Gospel Pass at slightly less than a walking pace. He was singing along to the Inkspots in a clear, Eisteddfod prize-winning tenor, mouthing in the spoken lulls.

– Yeah. Yeah. The night is cold. Yeah. For love is old. Yeah. That's what I thought. Yeah…

He turned in his seat, looking back towards the full moon close above the back of the Twmpa; then he flipped off the headlights.

Approaching the dark split between the mountains, PC Price tried to imagine the Inkspots in performance: the four of them, in a row onstage. They'd be black, of course; but black like black people used to be, before they were Naomi Campbell, and Ian Wright, and Lenny Henry, who were basically just the same as everyone else. The Inkspots would have been different. They'd have grinned unnaturally, contorted their bodies, looked out at the audience through fathomless eyes.

Reconstitute the bodies from the eyes, and there you'd have the truth of it. The Inkspots beneath the Inkspots – histories of love agony, slavery agony, suppression agony – an aching shackled by formality. That was why they sang so well. PC Price had for years had a conceit that proper black people and proper Welsh people amounted to very much the same thing; though for the sake of his professional reputation he did try and keep this to himself.

They were in unison now – PC Price and the Inkspots – their voices slipping into falsetto:

> *I'll find you in the morning sun,*
> *And when the night is new……*
> *I'll be looking at the moon,*
> *But I'll be seeing you.*

The piano and the backing vocals died away and the tape came, for the third time that day, to an end. In the silence, PC Price cleared his throat and switched off the stereo. He listened a moment to the gentle hum of the engine, then pressed his foot a little way down on the accelerator, gratified by the rise in pitch.

In the darkness, the walls of the Gospel Pass came apart like curtains. Swinging the wheel with the sudden right of the road, the moonlight caught PC Price's face: his pale skin, spotted with stubble and the blackness of sideburns, his disordered hair a mesh of shadows. He steered right again and ducked the car into a passing place.

The radio instructions had come through near the beginning of the tape's first side. Halfway through *Street of Dreams*, as it happened, which he'd been singing along to in his usual impassioned manner.

– PC 192. A male, Welsh voice. Come in, PC 192. Please confirm your location. Over.

PC Price was elsewhere, strolling down the sunny side of the Street, his best girl on his arm and a trilby tipped jauntily on his head. Now and then the two of them would perform a synchronised skip or spin which neither of them either prompted or acknowledged.

– Andy! said the voice, much louder. Oy! Andy! Where are you, boy?

PC Price snapped awake and reached hastily for the radio.

– PC 192, he stated. Continue. I was investigating a, er, suspicious-looking deserted vehicle.

– Were you hell, said the voice.

– I'm just outside Llanthony, said PC Price. On the Capel-y-ffin side.

– Got a bit of a job for you, Andy. Alright? You'll love this one.

– What's that, then?

– Get yourself up towards Hay Bluff, right? There's an ambulance up there – decommissioned ambulance, it is – about halfway across the common at the bottom, next to the road there. You can't miss it. They're broken down either ways, so they're not going to be going anywhere. Word is they're druggies or something. I dunno. Arrest them, yeah? There'll be an 'elicopter out to back you up.

PC Price thought a moment.

– What if they've got guns? he said.

– Aw, don't worry about it, boy. No-one'd be sending you up there if they'd got guns now, would they, eh?

170 – Alright, said PC Price uneagerly. I'm onto it.

The moon hadn't yet made it above Tarren yr Esgob, so the trees and fields and bracken were still in darkness. He loved this road at night. The way the Milky Way followed it, straight above the black arch of the valley.

Sure enough there was an ambulance down there, its paint bright against the grey ripples of the common, the shadow from the moon long behind it. Lights spotted the hills as far as PC Price could see.

Standing in the middle of the narrow road, he was watching the figures busying themselves on the common – forms only at this distance. Apparently they were involved in changing the left front wheel. They seemed too to be moving things from and into another vehicle parked behind the first. A car of some sort, although he couldn't see enough of it to determine what.

It was the same ambulance, though, that much he was sure of. And Colin had talked about people, not person, driving it. That meant there were others beside the freak with the dreadlocks and the eyes pointing in different directions, who had in fact struck him as an alright sort of bloke. Too obviously suspicious to really be dangerous. So far as he could make out, anyway, there were a good four people down there. Probably there were more in the vehicles.

Well, he was buggered if he was going to start wading in there with his truncheon. Even if he didn't get shot or assaulted or something, what the hell was he supposed to do with more criminals than there were seats in his car? And besides, the nearest open police station was in Brecon, which was well over half an hour's drive away; and he didn't even know what to charge them with even if he did manage to get them there. He'd been on duty now for thirteen hours one way or another. All he really wanted was a nice pint of Cointreau and lemonade down at the Wheatsheaf – which, he resolved, he would be going to get the moment this lot left.

PC Price walked back up the road towards the car, the slopes to either side of him sheer and in shadow. Sitting back in the driver's seat, he removed the Inkspots tape from the stereo, turned it over and pushed it back in again. There was a hissing

171

noise for a few seconds then the Inkspots' ubiquitous guitar intro ushered in the *Street of Dreams*:

> *Love laughs at a king.*
> *Kings don't mean a thing*
> *On the street of dreams…*

PC Price sang softly now, sighing with the runs of the piano, watching as the front wheels of the ambulance sank back to the ground. Someone was moving equipment – a jack, presumably, and a punctured wheel – then there was a splash of colour at the front of the car as its lights came on and it began to pull away across the grass, revealing itself as a Mark I Escort estate. It threw its light briefly on a man – quite tall, quite well-built – and a shapely young woman, who lifted a hand to wave at it.

The story he would shortly be leaking in the pub was beginning to take form in PC Price's mind. There were big-time London criminals hiding out around these parts – or on the loose, perhaps – wild-eyed lunatic men and beautiful-but-deadly women. For the first time that day he didn't sing along to *Home on the Range*, running through his lines instead.

– Course, I can't tell you any details, though I dare say you'll be reading a headline or two about it soon enough. And not in the *Brecon and Radnor* neither… And not just in the *Brecon and Radnor* neither. Oh, mine's a pint, Sid. Cheers.

172

– *…where seldom is heard a discouraging word.*

Colours were showing at the front of the ambulance too now. It shuddered a moment like it was trying to drive against the handbrake, then it began to roll forwards, turning right onto the lane, and, mercifully, taking another right rather than coming up towards the Gospel Pass where he would doubtlessly have been obliged to arrest them.

– 'Course, I saw them. Well, I saw them a couple of times, as it goes… Yeah. Chased them too. Christ knows what engine they've got in that van of theirs…! Oh, but you should see their women! Beautiful, they are! Fucking beautiful! Deadly too, of course. You got to watch them… Oh, ta, Joe. Cointreau… Lemonade. Anyway, I shouldn't really be telling you this…

Once *Home on the Range* had died back down to a hiss, PC Price restarted the Maestro, removing the radio from the dashboard.

– Colin, it's Andy. Come in, would you?

– Andy! What's going on? Do you require back-up?

– Got some, have you? Colin… Look. There was this tractor jack-knifed on the Capel-y-ffin road. Took a bit of time to get over here. There's no-one around. Some tracks that might have been theirs, but that's it, basically.

– Now that is a shame, Andy.

The two voices had much the same level of sincerity. PC Price released the handbrake and the Maestro began to roll down the hill.

– Isn't it? he said.

– Well, never mind. Nothing to be done. You'd best sign off for the day, then.

– That's just what I was planning, Colin. You have a good weekend, hey?

u: topiary

The trees made a tunnel around the ambulance: its headlights a circle on the walls, evolving with the twisting and pitch of the lane. Angus was driving, thinking about Ipswich, watching the hill as it fell away in front of them.

His sixth-form self had had straggly hair and smoked a lot of cigarettes. If he were to meet him now he was quite sure that he wouldn't like him: a sullen, drunken teenager who hung around derelict buildings when he wasn't out shoplifting.

There was one night, he remembered, when they'd got a few carloads of people together and went out to a castle on the coast. They'd had speakers, record-decks, petrol tanks, a generator and a box full of empty milk bottles, all of which they hoisted over a fence and arranged around the crumbling walls. Techno was the thing of the moment – the type with the rousing build-ups – so they put some on, jumping around and generally getting wasted till the first light grazed the clouds above the sea, and they gathered themselves round the well to drop petrol bombs.

Each of the bombs had had a circle of light on the walls around it, following it down. The circles had had a weight-lessness about them. Momentarily, they'd always made Angus wish to be falling too; then, just before the bottle hit the bottom, they'd turn into a dot and you'd have to jump backwards, glass, stones and dust shooting up into the air.

Fay was on the far side of the front seat, her hair in a curtain across her face, her feet in cleared spaces on the floor. She was looking through the window beside her.

The lane was getting tighter, slick with a sludge of leaves. Tim was in between them, smoking, rocking psychotically, occasionally talking to himself. In the back, Belle spoke only when she required another cigarette.

On the stereo, Neil Young was singing:

> *Oh, Isabella! Proud Isabella!*
> *They tore you down and ploughed you under…*

Angus didn't feel easy driving an ambulance; any easier than he would have done driving a hearse.

They stopped – just – when they arrived at the main road, the wheels slithering where a tractor had left mud around a gateway. Beyond the verge in front of them, the Wye was gorged and choppy, thinking itself still in the mountains. It sparkled as the headlights swung across it; then there was only the road – wide and flat and heavily subsidised by the European Union, leading to putative Toyota factories and tourist resorts that were sunny in the photos.

> *An ambulance can only go so fast.*
> *It's easy to get buried in the past,*
> *When you try to make a good thing last.*

Angus reached forward abruptly and pressed Eject; then he turned off the radio too – white noise humming at the pitch of the engine – and watched the road in silence. The song seemed to have been tapping his brain, broadcasting his thoughts with an acoustic guitar and a mournful, sliding fiddle.

– I was enjoying that, said Fay, without looking away from the window; a blurred line of houses, their doorsteps on the roadside.

– Sorry, said Angus. I was just finding it a bit, you know, bald… You couldn't put on anything a bit more upbeat, could you?

175

Fay bent down to pick up the tape bag, inspecting the titles in the moonlight. She dug out some brew of hip-hop and classical music, which he didn't recognise but somehow felt appropriate.

The moon was behind them when Angus first realised something was wrong, fields and hedges luminous to either side. At first he glanced at the instruments, pumping the accelerator, but soon he noticed steam, escaping from a side of the bonnet. He flipped on the indicator, swearing to himself and steering into a layby.

There was a mound of gravel higher than the roof on the ground before the hedge, one end of it mined by a digger. Not far away a phonebox glowed placidly. Tim smoked, staring with the beams of the headlights. Angus rubbed his eyes and turned off the ignition.

– What is it? said Fay.

– It might be my imagination, said Angus, but I think that the radiator's boiling.

– Ah yeah, the meter's bust, said Fay. It boiled last night too. I'm not sure how much water Pete put back in.

– Well, said Angus, sliding open the door and climbing out. I guess we're just going to have to sort it out.

Glancing back across the cab, his eyes met Fay's for a second or two. Their faces were both lit by the headlights, both tired and worried-looking, shadowed by hair. It made Angus feel glad and, at the same time, strangely defensive: glad that someone sane was around to help him, defensive because that look – the worriedness – had become a kind of domain for him. He wasn't sure that he was prepared or even knew how to share it.

The two of them stood, watching the steam as it slackened. The engine was plainly too hot to keep driving.

The track from Pentwyn arrived at the main road about a mile on from where the ambulance had broken down. If you were to look at a map – or if you were a bird – the little rectangle of the cottage would appear about equidistant between these two more-or-less-straight lines. They hadn't, of course, broken down on the nearest point of their particular axis, but the situation could have been a good deal worse. On the other side of the road was a stile and, as the occasional rambler served to prove, the footpath did pass the cottage's front door.

Angus led the way along the edge of a ploughed field, a tattered rucksack on his shoulder with badges from Bolivia and Colombia tacked all over it. Inside, poking into his back, were the tapes, Paolo's mobile, and a large grey ghetto blaster. The lines of the furrows stood out in moonlight and shadow. No-one was talking.

He waited when he got to the next stile, watching Belle as she slithered towards him. Tim had mud smeared down his right-hand side. Fay had her hands in the pockets of her fleece. Her hair was tied back. She walked along the verge carefully, elegantly.

– Jesus, muttered Belle, clambering over the stile. How much further?!

She steadied herself against Angus's shoulder then headed across a narrow footbridge on the other side, becoming catlike when she noticed the weed-covered pond beneath her.

Tim had his carrier bag clutched to his stomach, like an old woman with her handbag. He whimpered as Angus pushed him across the bridge, pointing him at the thick wet grass of the next field. Belle draped herself around Angus's neck, shivering, her right breast squashed indifferently against his chest.

The sky was clear and, until they came to the top of the field above the cottage, there were no lights visible in any direction. A wood passed to their left, the trees thick and

177

spindly, struggling sunwards and stifling one another in the process. Inside his mind Angus could still see the pinprick of whiteness: the burning's remnant, shining steadily.

– That's it, Belle, he said finally. You can do the rest on your own.

He moved her arm and let it fall against her side.

– Bastard, she muttered, turning to look down the tractor tracks towards the cottage at the bottom of the hill.

There were candles in lines along the kitchen and living-room windowsills, expanding window shapes issuing onto the wet ground. A ceremony of some sort might have been underway in there, an angel in attendance.

Belle lit another cigarette and began to walk towards it. Fay was twenty yards away – still – watching her.

– Say something, said Angus, when Belle was out of earshot.

The moon was behind him. Fay's face shone white with it.

– Your turn, she said. Her voice sounded constricted.

– Okay, he said. Well... I don't think you can see in daylight. How about that? You can only even begin to see at night.

Fay smiled faintly. She folded her arms across her chest and set off down the hill.

178   – Hello, my lovely! Had a bit of fresh air, have we? Yes...

Paolo, Pete and Nick were spread around the kitchen, apparently in an advanced state of shock. In place of the angel, Mrs Lloyd was grinning in a chair beside the roaring woodburner, a knackered-looking sheepdog on the floor beside her. She prised herself upright and headed across the room.

– Hello, Mrs Lloyd, said Angus.

– Aren't you going to introduce me to your friends, then? she said, planting a maternal kiss on his cheek.

– Er, sure, Angus stammered a moment. Mrs Lloyd. This is Fay. Belle. And, er, this is... Tim.

Mrs Lloyd looked closely at Fay, and Belle, but when she got to Tim she drew her head back sharply. He was shaking uncontrollably, one side of his face coated with mud, and his sunken eyes staring straight through her fleshy red head, its huge brown eyes, short black hair and unlikely lines of lipstick.

– Good Lord! said Mrs Lloyd, genuinely concerned. Are you alright?

– No, he's not, said Angus quickly. I... I think he's coming down with something.

– In fact, I was just about to put him to bed, said Fay.

She shepherded him towards the stairwell.

– Don't worry, Mrs Lloyd, said Angus. He just fell in some mud, and he's got a bit of a chill. That's all... Would you like a cup of tea at all?

– I've, er... I've got one, she said. Her eyes followed Tim across the room. Your friends here were very kind and put the kettle on...

She returned to her chair, made a visible effort to recover herself, then picked up her cup and sipped at it illustratively. With some relief, Angus realised that she'd been drinking.

– So, he said. What brings you down here?

– Well, said Mrs Lloyd, inhaling deeply. Philip met a couple of these lads here up in the yard this afternoon, so I thought to myself: You're going to have to get down to Hollow Cottage and see this with your own eyes! If Mr Angus Persey has some friends, well, it should be advertised! And I knew who that sounded like a job for... Besides, I was thinking: Where are these people going to wash and... attend to themselves? So I had a bit of a think, and I came up with an idea.

– Oh yes? said Angus, looking up as Fay reappeared at the bottom of the stairs.

179

– Is he okay, dear? asked Mrs Lloyd.

– Much better thankyou, said Fay. Nothing that a good night's sleep won't put right.

– That's good news! said Mrs Lloyd. I... I was just explaining to Angus here that my sister Ethel – Ethel runs the pub just over the hill from here. Sun Inn, it is. Very nice little pub – Well, they have campers there in the summer but, of course, there aren't any there at the minute, so I thought: Mary, those friends of Mr Persey down in Hollow Cottage might just appreciate a nice hot shower, not to mention making use of the, er, other facilities that Hollow Cottage isn't so hot on, so I gave Ethel a bell – I was ringing her anyway, like – and if you'd like to go over there tomorrow, well, that's fine by her. It's only five or ten minutes over the hill...

Nick had the Vladivar bottle on his lap and was frowning, staring around the room. Paolo was looking at what appeared to be a miniature hedgerow, woven from twigs on the table in front of him. Pete was cross-legged on the rug in front of the woodburner, resuming fiddling with vegetable and flesh sausages, two tins of baked beans and seven foil-wrapped potatoes in the fire. Belle put an arm around his shoulder, shivering pointedly. There was a trail of mud behind her, like snail slime.

180

– Who the... motherfuck was that?! said Nick eventually.

– That was Mrs Lloyd, said Angus. The landlady. Nick. Is that bottle empty?!

– Er, yeah, Nick admitted. Sorry. Have you got any more?

– No, I haven't! Angus dropped Pete's rucksack behind the door and sank into a chair. Jesus, Nick! That was the last bottle!

– Angus has been horrible to me, Belle confided to Pete.

– Oh! said Nick, spotting the stereo in the neck of the rucksack.

– Where the hell have yous lot been, anyway? said Pete. Yous've been gone for hours.

– Yeah, said Angus. Well, the radiator boiled on the main road, so we had to leave it in a layby… And we got a puncture on the hill. So it's all taken quite a long time.

Everyone stopped talking, except Belle, who was still trying to extract sympathy out of Pete. Then Nick began busily setting up the stereo on the sideboard. Paolo picked up his hedge and resumed work on it.

– Jesus! said Angus. It's not like we meant to.

– That's a bummer, said Paolo. Basically.

– What happened to the spare, Pete? said Fay.

There was a blast of very hard trance from the stereo. Nick turned it down hurriedly.

– There's one in the back, said Pete. Under the futon.

– No, there isn't, said Angus. The compartment's empty… We looked everywhere.

The music was thundering along at 150 bpm, various *Peoww!* noises darting across the top of it. Fay went through to the utility room, still worried-looking. There was the squeak – then rush – of the tap as she set about washing her hands.

– Christ! said Pete, more confused than anything.

– Porco Giuda! said Paolo phlegmatically. Sounds like you've had a bit of a time… Tell you what. I'll take some water over to it now and drive it back to the yard. It was all of us who should have remembered to fill it up, after all.

Pete looked at him, his left eye running over the bruise on the side of his face.

– Paolo, he said. I don't want to seem suspicious, but… you want to walk all the way out to the main road in the dark and fill up the radiator two minutes before supper?! I mean, you've been rolling me joints and making me cups of tea all day! Maybe you want to drive down the Congo, huh? Civilise a few natives…

– Yeah, said Paolo. Why don't you just rub it in? Why don't you just fucking rub it in? Look… I'm glad we came, I really am. But, if you remember, it was me who talked about dealing on the phone. It was me who made everyone leave the house and drive across the country all night… I feel bad about it! Okay? I was trying to make it up!

It was strange. Angus didn't want Fay to look worried. It made him want to wash his own hands or, at any rate, do the equivalent: drink himself into a stupor or vanish into his story, or preferably both. If Fay would just look happy – the way she had on the hill – he knew that some sort of burden would evaporate. Whether it was a new burden, or the same old burden just dressed up differently, he really didn't know. He didn't really care either. He just wanted rid of it.

Angus brought his desk into the middle of the room, pushing it up against the kitchen table before blocking the two level. Fay returned from the utility room, covering them with an off-white curtain and arranging the plates and cutlery while he went around blowing out candles for the sake of economy and moving a couple onto the table by way of garnish.

– Do you want food, Tim? Pete shouted up the stairwell.

Tim didn't reply, so he spooned out the beans six ways: to Belle, who had sat herself at the head, then to Nick and Paolo on one side, and Fay and Angus who were on the side and the other head respectively, their knees almost touching.

– Evenin', said Angus, hoping that he might make her smile.

Fay did smile, faintly – like she had in the field – but she still didn't say anything.

It was more than a burden. The worry was different to the blinding affliction of the past few months. Fay's eyes were on her plate. She looked so troubled, Angus realised, that he wanted to cheer her up for her own sake as much as for his own.

They all had a potato split open with a daub of long-life margarine in its middle, convincingly butter-like in the candlelight. On the woodburner the sausages were spitting noisily, blackened and smelling tasty.

– Sausages for you, Paolo? said Pete conciliatorily.

Paolo was inspecting his fork.

– I'll have the vegetable ones, he said. Please.

– There's not enough, said Pete. Paolo… You know we only got them for me and Belle.

– Then I'll have none, said Paolo.

– Oh, for Christ's sake, said Pete. You always have meat!

The look on Paolo's face was intense enough for Pete to rub his hand on his forehead and give up. He spooned a couple of the vegetable ones onto Belle's plate, which she sniffed at critically.

Fay smiled faintly again when she received her sausages.

– Ta, she said.

– No worries, said Pete.

He served himself last, his piercings glinting in the candlelight, then he reached for the salt pot, sprinkling it liberally over his plate.

183

Fay, Angus realised, was looking at him from a corner of her eye. He waited for a second or two, then cautiously looked back. She turned away at once, but in the split second their eyes did meet something seemed to fall into place.

He saw her, and he saw the Fay that he'd known in Kingston, and he saw both of them in the Fay that he'd been with on the hill that afternoon. The two were like constricted versions: semi-deliberate projections that would probably fool you indefinitely, so long as you'd never seen the real thing.

— I think, said Angus, finishing a sausage, that I might go and lie down for a bit. Could anyone, er, lend us a fag?

Pete held out a packet.

— I thought you'd given up, said Fay quietly.

— Yeah, said Angus. I had.

v: you damned

It was an instant. We were nearing the southernmost tip of
Okinawa, the formation banked precisely for the approach
to Kerama-retto. To our right there were lights on the
coastline: Yonabaru and, isolated further south, villages,
households, fires and bolts of mirrored moonlight. The shore
was a pale streak between the dense subtropical undergrowth
and the blackness of the Pacific. Waves were threads of
whiteness – twined and untwined – frozen in the limits of my
right eye. In the window to my left, the moon was a single,
immediate reflection. Before me the Zeroes were still in their
impaired arrangement, thirty degrees from the horizontal as
we turned towards the west, when on the far side of the
formation the propeller blades of a Zero faltered.

All five of us understood that any laden Zero departing
from Oita would find Kerama-retto at the very extent of its
range; that if one propeller were to falter, then, soon enough,
others would certainly follow.

The Zero to my right lost impetus sharply, caught like a
leaf by the rules of the passing world, falling from its place
and lapsing behind us, with a crack! from the headphones and
a cry of such volume and anguish that the radio must almost
have burst from it.

The cry was terminated by a short, concrete blow; in my
mind, a little patch of moonlight white on the endless surface
of the ocean. Yet it was as significant to me as the sun-
brilliant blasts of the A-bombs themselves. The target was

eighty kilometres westwards: twenty minutes at our laden velocity. I rolled my eyes towards the fuel gauge – the needle leaning left – then to the artificial horizon where a pair of pictured wings were returning to a level.

The five of us were scattered across the sky, the south coast of Okinawa to our right and the Earth in shadow around us.

– Alright? Pete was standing in the mouth of the stairwell, a hand on each jamb.

– Huh? said Angus, looking up.

– The cigarette…

– Oh. Angus rolled the half-smoked Marlboro between two fingers, then dropped it into the ashtray. Pretty fucking horrible to tell you the truth.

Pete removed his hands and glancing, not entirely easily, across the porcelain and crumbling plaster, he wandered over to the end of the bed and sat down. He swung his legs up so they ran parallel to Angus's.

– What you up to? he asked, one-eyeing the pile of A4 paper on his lap.

– I'm, er, just writing this story… said Angus.

Pete raised his eyebrows in an expression of interest. He pulled a pre-rolled joint from a pocket of his khaki combats and lit it, leaning back against the bed-end.

– It's… Angus thought a moment. It's about this kamikaze mission that happened after the end of the Second World War, after the Japanese surrender. A squadron went from Kyushu to crash into the US fleet, as a final act of defiance, but… they vanished. You know? No-one knows where they went.

Pete blew a couple of meditative smoke-rings.

– Fuck of a way to go, he said.

– The thing is, said Angus, when the Japanese Emperor declared surrender on the radio, that was the first time he'd ever been heard by his subjects, you know? He was a God. He was invincible. So the first time that he spoke to his subjects he was effectively denying his own divinity.

Pete frowned. His dreadlocks were loose down the sides of his face, the candles shining on his piercings and picking out the shadows on his temples: two principally, converging into a V shape between his eyebrows.

– Dying for a dead divinity, he said. Poor sods... What were they? Like, twenty or something?

– Yeah, nineteen or twenty, most of them. I mean, in some ways they were still like children. Their identities were so bound up in their culture that when the surrender came – you know? – either they gave up their spirit, or else they had to kill themselves.

– Kamikazed either way... Pete murmured.

Angus tapped the joint on the rim of the candlestick. He sucked on it cautiously.

– Yeah, he said. I guess so. You know what kamikaze means, yeah? Divine wind... Like, twice in the thirteenth century, the Mongolians tried to invade the Japanese islands, and both times a typhoon blew up and wiped out the entire fleet... The idea in the Second World War was to do the same thing to the Americans, except using humans, of course.

Angus's head was spinning. He took another puff on the joint and handed it back to Pete, trying to pull his thoughts together.

– Incidentally, said Pete a moment later, I did come up here for a reason. Like, you were looking kind of freaked out downstairs. You, er... You talked to Belle today?

– Ah, yeah, said Angus. Yeah. Whether she heard me or not I don't know, but I did talk to her... You know about Rob, I suppose?

187

– I surmised about Rob, said Pete tactfully, dropping the roach into a tea cup, tapping his toes to the funk music coming up the stairwell.

– Yeah. Angus smiled weakly. Well. Belle was so off her face she probably didn't even know what was going on. But it's not a problem. You know? Suddenly. Not like I thought it'd be... Something happened up there. Something sorted itself out, though I haven't quite figured out what. Besides, there's other things to think about for once.

– Like? Pete raised an eyebrow. He was rolling a scrumpled ball of paper around the palm of his right hand.

– Like... Angus hesitated. Well, like everyone turning up here, for a start. This raid. Whatever...

– Ah yeah, said Pete. Yeah. There's something to think about.

– How do you mean? said Angus.

– Aggh! shrieked Belle, through the funk and the ceiling. A moth! Get it away from me! It'll go in my ear!

Pete had an absorbed look on his face. He gripped the stud in his lower lip between his teeth.

– Well, said Pete. I don't know. It's just a gut thing, but... well, basically I think Paolo knows something. I mean, more than he says. Maybe Nick does too. The thing is, though, realistically, what? Like, okay, Paolo gets enthusiastic about peculiar things and that. But what could he possibly be up to that's worse than what the rest of us get up to the whole time anyway?

For a moment the two of them sat in silence, both with their arms folded.

– Except, he said, there is this one thing I keep coming back to. When the house got raided, this pig told me they thought we had an acid factory... I mean, I know it sounds daft, and I'm not saying they've got one under the bed or anything. But, I just got this feeling that there was something behind it. Like, the pigs knew something about them but couldn't prove it, or Paolo and Nick do know who's actually got it and can't say anything, or… I mean, they looked scared as fuck during that raid. Do you know what I mean? Paolo never looks scared.

Angus nodded slowly.

– Well, he said, I'll try and keep my ears open.

Angus felt better, having talked to Pete. When he'd gone back down the stairwell he stayed where he was, propped against the bedhead: calm – tentatively – sparse fractals evolving inside his eyelids.

Snippets of conversation were creeping in between his thoughts.

– No, really! Well, it was my great-uncle, I think. A moth got into his ear and started eating his brain. It couldn't get back out.

– Yeah, his brain… scoffed Paolo.

– Really! Belle insisted. It ate some of the numerative part! He was never able to add up odd numbers again!

Silence was hanging over the cottage, defiant to the voices and the Meters on the stereo. There were other sounds too, upstairs. The wind in the trees. The stream, growing prominent the moment you noticed it, like a clock, ticking away in a sleeping household – less a noise somehow than a foil to the wider silence.

– A fish, though?! Jesus Christ!

Nick and Paolo walked past him, entering the spare bedroom, Nick quarrelling drunkenly about mattresses.

Once they'd settled and the door between them was closed, Angus reopened his eyes and took the half-cigarette from the candlestick beside him. Someone was turning the volume down slowly on the stereo, till finally it was silent and the sounds from outside began to assert themselves. Downstairs Pete seemed to have made his bed on the chaise longue. There were Goodnights, the roar of the tap, then – Angus shut his eyes again – Belle's footsteps creeping up the stairs, becoming almost silent as they passed him.

Fay too, it seemed, was sleeping downstairs. There was no further noise beside the odd drunken snore or witty comment through the wall behind him; so, taking the half-cigarette, Angus resumed his seat on the rug beside the window, sitting cross-legged and watching the moon, close above the nub of Llandefalle.

There were cirrocumuli across the western quarter of the sky – ripplings that made the moon seem even milkier. At the top of the field were the stark silhouettes of trees. Then, quietly, the front door swung open and Fay walked out onto the grass, Nick's hat pulled down on her head and his old green coat wrapped tight around her. He watched – still not lighting the cigarette – as she stepped carefully over the end of the fence, and set off up the hill towards the wood.

w: under the moon

As a non-Christian recluse, it always surprised Angus how much he was able to wring out of a Sunday morning. It was the only time when he'd have absolutely no guilt at all about anything. There'd be the formless warmth of the bedclothes, enough awareness to understand it was a Sunday; and that, for once, would be all there was to it.

The business of prolonging this condition had, over the past few months, developed into a bit of an artform: a delicate balancing act that any sort of disturbance could scupper immediately. So ideally he needed no rain, a light breeze, and the nose alone exposed to the room outside. There was more to this than crankiness. A mile away, at around nine o'clock on a Sunday morning, the bellringers of Boughrood would burst into activity, providing Angus's sole direct contact with regular human society – shopping excepted – and music too, for that matter. Under perfect conditions, the breeze would have him steeled against the notion of sudden sounds while the bells wandered into a dream's background, easing him awake with a volume much like the stream's. The fractured runs, in fact, did sound a lot like water. Running water, that is. Not rain, which just eclipsed everything.

This morning, thankfully, it was not raining. Indeed, there was something in the breeze to suggest it was sunny again. Way off in the distance the bells were rippling jerkily down a major scale, the stream talking away beneath them. The two might almost have been a single music and, for some reason, they were tirelessly evoking an image of Fay: on the riverbank that day they first moved into the house in Kingston.

It was in this reverie – drifting along at any easy pace – that Angus first became aware of a popping, crackling noise. Instantly the half-sleep was shattered. He sprang upright, blinking, dragging himself across the bed towards the sounds of fire, remembering the houseful of people only as his feet touched the floor.

Someone had lit the woodburner. That was all. For a moment Angus sat there, absorbing the surprise, the pleasure when he'd settled something deeper than relief.

A few minutes later Angus found himself quite taken with the idea of getting up. He shuffled down the bed till his head was adjacent to the window, looking out across the wheat stubble, the few sheep picking at weeds about halfway towards the horizon, the scraps of greyish cloud passing west through an otherwise pristine sky.

Perched in the elder tree about four feet away, a squirrel was watching him; their eyes met through the thin glass. The squirrels' eyes were feral. More so at least than the mouse's the previous morning. Angus stuck his tongue out at it and pulled himself over to the other side of the bed.

192   The church bells were clearly audible as he trod down the stairs. The flagstones seeped cold into the soles of his feet. There were smells: woodsmoke, mouse shit, dust, damp.

Tim had his back to him. He was standing on the rug beside the woodburner, a china basin of steaming water on a chair to his right, soap in his one hand and a rag in the other. He was wearing only a pair of Y-fronts, his back and legs sagging like they'd been left to him by someone much larger. He appeared to be lost in the sound of the fire, his head hanging forward.

Across the lower part of his back a cluster of thin, deep scars ran down into his Y-fronts, cut into the flesh so nubs of vertebrae stuck out white against the scar tissue.

– Er... said Angus.

Tim span round. He grabbed at a T-shirt, concealing a chest like an old man's.

– Oh. Ah... Alright, Angus?

– Alright, Tim. Angus glanced around the room. Carry on, huh? I was just going to do a bit of tidying up. You know. I shan't look.

– Oh. No, said Tim. No. I was just finished. Sorry. I... I thought everyone was asleep.

Tim's face seemed dangerously grey. His eyes were sunken and bewildered. He was almost falling as he fought with his mud-spattered jeans and the T-shirt, which read *E-Z* in day-glo lettering.

– Tim? said Angus, crossing the room and starting to assemble a pile of dishes. I hope you don't mind me asking, but those scars on your back? What the hell happened?

– Oh, said Tim. Just, er... Just some shit one time. I fell through a window.

Angus looked at him, and remembered something Pete had said once, about meeting someone who'd known Tim at school. He'd been fat back then, apparently, and pretty badly bullied. It had only stopped when someone pushed him through a plate-glass window, when his parents had moved him to somewhere else.

– It's, er, no big deal... said Tim, seeing the expression on Angus's face. It was just an accident. Ages ago.

When Paolo and Nick came crashing downstairs about half an hour later, Angus was clean-shaven, his hair brushed back from

193

his forehead with a decent pair of combats on and a fresh, tight black T-shirt.

The kitchen was tidy: the flagstones swept, the plates, cutlery and saucepans washed and put away, the new tablecloth shaken clean outside before being replaced on the newly arranged table. The door was open so they could hear the church bells when they resumed.

– What? Nick was stammering, a T-shirt halfway onto his fleshless frame. What the fuck?!

– We're going to move the ambulance, hissed Paolo as they arrived in the kitchen.

– What the fuck do you want with me? Nick whimpered. My head! You've no fucking idea…!

He collapsed into a chair, grimacing and doubling over. Angus selected a large, particularly elaborate teapot from the shelf – Broad Way Victorians strolling all over it – throwing in a couple of tea bags and filling it with boiling water.

– I'll have some tea ready in a minute, he said. If you want some…

– Tea! croaked Nick.

– No! said Paolo.

– What's the fucking hurry…?!

Paolo said nothing. He was scowling, twisting a piece of hair at the front of his ramshackle Afro, peering around the room. He was still wearing the clothes from the day before – the muddy, crumpled flares and cheesecloth shirt – and for the first time Angus could remember, his endless stubble had finally turned into a beard.

– What are you after? said Angus.

– Keys… said Paolo. Ambulance keys.

Angus pointed to a hook on the right-hand doorpost, and Paolo exhaled gently, going over and stuffing them in his pocket.

They were halfway across the field when Paolo resumed talking, a scribbled map in his right hand and the sleeve of Nick's T-shirt in his left.

– Nick, he said. Che cazzo! What the fuck is the matter with you, huh?! You ask what the fuck the hurry is in front of the others?!... Never! Fucking never do that again!

– What? Nick was stumbling on ruts in the stubble, breathing so hard he could barely speak.

– What?! Paolo echoed. Fucking What?! You heard what I said, dickhead! Never fucking question me in front of them like that!

– Why the fuck not? Nick managed. I'll do what I like.

– From now on, said Paolo, you'll do what I fucking want you to do. Get it? Every time you do something alone it goes wrong. So leave it to me...

A group of sheep scattered as they approached the top of the field, becoming unsure, having retreated twenty feet or so, whether they should in fact be following them. So they stood exactly where they were, watching as Paolo opened the gate, heading towards the spindly, balding mass of the wood.

– I'm sitting down, said Nick a moment later, sitting down.

– Nick! Paolo massaged his forehead, turning back to look at him. Nick... Vaffanculo! This is your fucking life we're talking about here!

– What the fuck is wrong with you? said Nick, recovering   195
his breath slightly and squinting back at him from the thick grass. What the fuck is wrong with you, anyway? If you remember, we came out here so no-one would know where we are...?!

– Porco Guida! said Paolo. If you remember, shit-for-brains, you left a note behind!

– I left, said Nick – an edge of Clapton steeliness creeping into his voice – a note to Sonn saying that we'd gone to Ang's.

Yeah? Not we've gone to this fucking cottage, near this fucking village, in this fucking... Wales! So even if they did find it, they'd still have no idea where we are!

– Nick! How fucking stupid...? Who the fuck do you think we're playing with here? This is Steve Fisk! The man knows everyone! If anybody knows where we are – and Sonia bloody well does – then... face it, sooner or later Steve is going to find out.

– What...? said Nick. He pulled himself back up to his feet, his eyes creeping open.

– Well, what's he going to do...?! We know enough to send him down for the best part of his life and he thinks that's what we're trying. Not to mention the fact we've got acid worth probably a million quid to him or something. Face it! Him, or someone, is going to track down anyone who knows us, then come out here and look for the fucking ambulance...!

– Paolo! said Nick, his voice and face suddenly hardened. You fucking... bastard! You knew they'd go after Sonia, no matter what happened?!

– Nick... Paolo sighed. I didn't know shit, okay? What's done is done. Let's just move the fucking ambulance...?

He turned and set off towards a gate beside the trees ahead of them, walking quickly for four or five seconds before glancing back at Nick, who hadn't moved. He stopped again, opening his mouth to speak.

– Paolo! Nick snarled first. You'd better fucking well explain yourself now or that's it, I'm not going any further.

– Shit, Nick! Steve is not a friend of mine, huh?! He is a very nasty and a very dangerous man who will do anything necessary to get what he wants! Just, use your fucking head...!

– Phone, said Nick, extending his left hand, his shoulders back and square. Give me your phone, Paolo. I want to talk to her.

He took several steps forward. Paolo's face lost a shade of panicked colour.

– Nick?! he said. Do you not understand?! We have to do this now! Now, you fucking… heathen! This fucking second!

The two of them were face to face, Nick's left hand still extended and his right reaching down into his pocket. In slightly less than a second he'd produced the flick-knife, released the blade and pressed the tip to the visibly pulsing jugular in Paolo's neck.

– Nick, said Paolo, without flinching. For the sake… Put… Put that fucking thing away. We'll find a phonebox. Whatever… We'll drive to one! You know you can't use my phone.

A speck of blood had appeared at the end of the blade. It escaped and ran down into Paolo's chest hair. Paolo winced and tried to raise his hand but Nick moved forward for additional leverage and he left it hanging in the air.

– Nick, he said. Nothing might have happened, at all. Everything might be cool. We might get our money, and I might get my Ducati and… everyone might live happily ever after, but I swear, if you use that phone they'll send the fucking pigs in! They'll lock us up for fucking ever!

– Phone, said Nick again, his voice calm, twisting the knife slightly so another current of blood cascaded from Paolo's neck. You don't have to worry. I know what I'm doing. It takes them thirty seconds to locate a mobile call… I'm going to be less than that.

197

Belle appeared around the corner at the bottom of the stairwell, stopping and leaning against the inner wall: pushing her chest outwards then allowing it to fall back, raising her thumb to her lips, holding it there a second and finally inserting it. She looked at Angus across the room, doe-eyed but apparently uncertain what to do next.

– Do you want tea, then? said Angus, glancing at the receding figures of Nick and Paolo through the open door.

Belle removed her thumb.

– Um… alright, she said, smiling weakly and wandering over to the nearest chair, where she sat down.

– Uggh? said Tim invitingly from the corner, holding out the joint towards her.

Angus had forgotten he was there.

Belle smiled weakly again, receiving the joint and smoking it with a kind of wine-bar poise. Her jaw was still working from the previous day.

Through the door, Paolo was pretty much dragging Nick by the right sleeve of his T-shirt, Nick's feet sliding on the muddy ruts tramlining the field.

– So, I'm going to need to go to this pub… said Belle. Could you tell me how to get there?

– Yeah, said Angus, handing her the tea. He tried, without a glimmer of success, to imagine being close to her again. Yeah. It's really not far at all. I mean. if you go over the fields. I'll go up the hill with you in a minute, if you like; show you the path…

– Do you think they'll accept my credit card?

Belle had become little-girl-like suddenly, as she did sometimes. Her thumb was back beneath her mouth.

– Why? What do you need?

– I… I just thought I might want to spend some money on something.

Belle looked at him perplexedly. Angus finished his cup of tea and carried the cup through to the sink. The sounds of hawking came from the other downstairs room, then the scratch of a Zippo as Pete tried to light a cigarette.

– Pete! said Angus at the intervening door. You want to go to the pub?

There was another barrage of coughing.

– Yeah, he spluttered. Give us one minute, yeah?

A couple of crashes and further coughs brought Pete blinking into the kitchen, the end of a roll-up poking from a corner of his mouth and both hands tying his dreads into an onion effect on top of his head.

– Ah, tea! he muttered, heading towards the teapot and eyeing the gaily-clad ladies and gentlemen promenading round it. Jesus, this place is in a bloody timewarp...

Angus peered past him as discreetly as he could, looking over the cushions in the corner and the six foot of packing foam that lined the right-hand wall. Fay wasn't in there.

– Pete, he said. Where's Fay got to? I thought she was sleeping down here last night.

– Fay... said Pete slowly. He looked up from the UHT milk carton. Mmm. I think she's upstairs. I saw her last night; she went to bed very late. I'd, er... I'd leave her to sleep a bit if I was you.

His left eye held Angus's – pointedly – for a second or two; then he was slugging back tea, inviting Belle to pass him the joint, preparing himself to walk to the Sun.

x: the moth acts first...

The sun was low above the rock and tawny bracken of the hill behind Pentwyn. Tattered clouds and shadows flowed across the valley: over the concave fields, the farm, the cottage, the stubble-coated field, and Angus, sitting on a gate at its top. Some way down the hill behind him, Pete, Tim and Belle were heading for the cluster of trees that marked the local pub. The clouds were following them, continuing to ford the river before scaling Llandefalle and setting a course for Cork.

Angus would come here quite often, watching or writing. When the cylindrical bales were in the field he'd sit cross-legged on one of those. These days he'd taken to sitting on the gate instead, observing the sheep. He'd pick one out at random and impose a characteristic on it: caddishness, for instance. Then, as it met with different situations, he'd test the characteristic against its responses, working the sheep out for itself.

He unfolded a piece of paper, and flattened it out on his thigh.

> *The last of our companions fell suddenly, the nose of his Zero catching a wave, the tail arcing onwards like a sperm whale's, vanishing in an explosion of moon-white spray.*
>
> *I flinched as the water broke against my canopy, parting in shivering strands. We were metres above the Pacific now, the rush of the swell audible despite the roar of our engines. The islands were in silhouette, trees gangling higher than our*

radio masts. Ahead was the target: a seaborne city, illuminated in celebration.

Searchlights were appearing among the colors and lanterns of victory: great, hard beams craning unsteadily across the water towards us, greens springing from the islands they touched and grays from the heaving sea.

In the seconds before the guns, every thought, every piece of knowledge grew effaced from my mind. Words detached from meaning seemed to ricochet about the cockpit: Emptiness, Invincibility, Sun, Substance, Zero, Sacrifice, Moon... Then there were only the relentless instants. The petrifying purity. The terror pinning the joystick to its course.

The Vice-Admiral banked northwards, tracer streaking past the bomb beneath him and his sights levelling on the flagship. Tiny, expanding figures chased from cover to cover, clutching weapons: one crumpling as the 20mm cannons and the 27.7mm machine guns opened upon him. Sparks flew from the fighters lining the flightdeck. Flames. Flickering lines of light radiated around us. I banked in turn – the aerolons sluggish with bullet-holes – the hulking mass of the carrier swelling before us.

– Activate! came the screamed instruction. Activate!

I flicked the switch that primed the bomb. My hand moved independently so fire burst from the nose of the Zero, strafing the hull, sending a pallid-faced man at the rail into spasms.

– TENNO HEIKA...!

The Vice-Admiral climbed sharply towards the deck, his cry continuing. Machine-gun fire burst the canopy around me. Air whipped my face, revived something in the numbness of my mind, drove the tears backwards from my eyes.

– BANZAI! he screamed. Weeping too. His conviction absolute to the very last moment.

The Vice-Admiral's Zero rose before me, sailing through the storm of the machine guns, coming level with the deck *graceful as a wide-winged bird; then the propeller faltered, finally. The scream continued, but the lost thrust brought a drop in trajectory. And in a space between instants, the Vice-Admiral became a fireball, minor against the huge black hull, doused in a second by the waves.*

The lights and fire were on me alone now, blinding as I climbed, cannon and machine guns cutting a path before me. Sensation was returning to my hands, to my arms and feet and head. I recalled myself as a child: mobs of us streaming down streets of wood and plaster houses.

– TENNO HEIKA!

I recalled cuckoos and fireflies on humid summer nights. The face of my mother, her young, dark eyes looking down on me.

– BANZAI! I screamed.

My voice was plucked by the wind, torn as the static had the Emperor's. Every muscle was rigid, holding the shredding Zero to its course. The propeller was faltering, the war in my hands now.

The conning-tower reared before me.

Shadows drifted on across the concave fields, the stream, the cottage, the mottling of weeds in the stubble. A couple of sheep were twenty feet away, heads up, observing Angus with dark inscrutable eyes like they could switch on luminance any time they felt like it. Air flowed across his face. The sun brought reds and yellows, greens, browns and oranges from the valley.

All morning, Fay had been there. And the night before. Angus was acknowledging it now, unsure when the feeling had started but unsure too that it really ever had. What, after all, had he been yearning for all these months?

The night before, when he'd caught Fay's eye at the table: that had been the moment. Her face had been pale again,

202

moon-white. He'd recognised her like you might recognise yourself in a photograph.

He put a hand through his again-dishevelled hair, filed a thumbnail between two teeth, played a hip-hop beat weakly on the top bar of the gate, then took it in both hands and sprang himself forward, landing in a sheep-beheaded patch of weeds.

Angus still walked around the field like the wheat was navel-high, following the tracks of the tractors, making right-angle turns where they intersected and there was nothing to stop you turning any way you liked. He headed straight down the hill, dodging puddles, watching smoke billow westwards from the cottage chimney. Everywhere the colours were beyond themselves, like those at the peak of sunset.

He stepped onto the overgrown lawn. His hand was shaking as he placed it on a fence post. He walked quietly towards the door, smoothing his hair down carefully and brushing out the wrinkles in his T-shirt, taking the latch and pushing the door away from him.

Colour spread in a wave across Fay's face. She dropped the paper back in the box in the corner, stepping away from it, wrapping her arms around her shoulders instinctively.

Her eyes had a grief-like intensity.

– Er… Sorry, she started. I… I just happened to see it.   203

Angus looked at her, then down at the flagstones, then back up at her again. She was so beautiful he could scarcely breathe, although it only seemed now that he was aware of it. The curve of her hips, her tied-back hair, the thin, uncovered angles of her shoulders.

– It's… okay, said Angus.

In the bottom of his vision, he could see his hands shaking. He kept thinking he should reverse but it was like climbing against a waterfall. The fact of her! It was all he could do to stay where he was.

– Er, said Fay. Could I ask you something?

– Okay, said Angus.

– That word. Banzai... What does it mean?

– It's, er... Angus cleared his throat. Well, it's... it's like a prayer for the Emperor. It's... Well, literally it means ten thousand years of life to you, but that's more a manner of speaking. Really, it means forever...

Fay smiled slightly. She shuffled, looking at him properly now.

– Um... she said. Can I ask you something else?

– Okay, said Angus.

– Would you come here, please?

Their eyes met again. Hers were fearful still, but there was certainty in there too. Then whatever had been holding him back evaporated. He moved forward, taking her head in his hands – their eyes staying locked for a second or two; then all four of them closed – and their lips met in the space between them.

Angus felt like he'd spent a lifetime orbiting a lightbulb – blinded, breaking himself against it – when all along the moon had been just beyond the open window. He felt like there was emptiness after all, but an emptiness in the places that, for some reason, he'd been certain he would find something.

The stiffness went out of Fay's body as they kissed – it did from his, too – and bit by bit he began to see what she'd been talking about, up on the hill. She'd understood him, he saw that now. He'd been clinging to another person's idea of himself and, finally, he was letting it go.

y: listen to the voice of doom.
open your eyes, blind fools!

– If you ask me, said Paolo, it was not a bad compromise. He shrugged, gesturing with the flick-knife. I mean, she's alive, right? And even I could hear her voice when she answered, so obviously she still loves you.

Nick's feet were slithering on the verge, slipping into the field's nearest furrow. He didn't reply.

– I mean, I just didn't trust that thirty second thing, Paolo went on. It's like, you could have got it from anywhere… *NYPD Blue* or *The Bill* or… you know. Anywhere. You've got to admit. Ten or twelve seconds was much safer?

He glanced back at Nick and, ensuring he wasn't watching, retracted the blade of the flick-knife and slid it into his waistband. Then he removed the phone from a pocket of his flares, weighing it a second before detaching the battery and hurling it halfway across the ploughed field, where it vanished into the mud.

– Cos we'd have gone to prison otherwise, he said. They'd have been straight out here and nailed us.

– They found her, said Nick suddenly. He looked up, squinting. A bruise distorted the left-hand side of his jawline. They found Sonia. They made her tell them where we are. They're going to kill us.

Paolo came to a halt.

– Oh, Jesus, he said.

A cloud shadow flickered west through the hedge on their right-hand side, covering them and progressing in instants over the crosswise furrows.

– Is… Is she alright?

– Like you give a shit!

– Nick?!

– She's alive, said Nick. Okay? She's in one piece.

– Jesus… said Paolo again. Shit!

He glanced at the stile and the otherwise impenetrable hedge that lined the main road in front of them. A car blinked from left to right of the opening. Across the road, crows swirled like leaves above a pine wood.

– Alright, he said eventually. Well, I… We… Here, have this back.

Paolo held the knife out, allowing Nick to take it and push it peremptorily back into his own waistband – below the navel, where the police didn't tend to look. He then went to the stile, leaning carefully over it and peering round the edge of the hedge.

The ambulance was in a layby about a hundred yards away, glowing grubby white. Paolo watched for several seconds, looking down the long smooth straightness of the road, at the hedges, the mountain of gravel, the phonebox.

– I think it's alright… he said.

Fay was still in a state of total amazement, kissing Angus, her arms around his back, the hardness of his crotch pressed against her. She was amazed by his excitement; she was amazed by the fact that it was happening at all.

She kept grinning uncontrollably.

Half the night she'd been walking round fields, trying not to think about him. Angus's hand was travelling down her back, settling on the curve at its base: she glowed where he touched her. She'd pictured herself going back down to Kingston, getting on with the course, maybe seeing him socially in another three months' time.

Neither of them heard the others till they were halfway across the lawn: Pete coughing smokily, Belle protesting about something to do with hygiene. They sprang apart immediately, Angus's face flushed as he stumbled against a chair, his pectorals prominent through his T-shirt, unsure quite where to look.

– Er... Alright? he said, as the door swung open. Nice... walk?

Pete looked from one of them to the other, opening his mouth but hesitating to say anything. Belle pushed past him, aiming for a stray packet of cigarettes on the table. She glanced up at Angus, then she looked at Fay.

A line appeared on her forehead.

Her eyes were big and mascaraed, her hair loose down the sides of her face, her lips slightly open. It made Fay turn cold.

– Fine, said Pete hurriedly. How are yous?

– Angus?! said Belle.

Tim wandered obliviously in from the garden, peering among empty tea cups and scattered cassettes on the sideboard before heading towards the stairwell.

– You're not even going to say anything?! Belle wrapped her pink cardigan tight around herself. Her voice was cracking. I... Angus? I... I can't believe you!

For a moment she was staring at them; then she spun and stormed outside, slamming the door behind her.

207

– Okay, said a voice to the left. Open the door, step back and throw me the keys...

Paolo was standing beside the driver's door of the ambulance, the keys in his hand. Suddenly he felt sick, his throat had shrunk so his breathing rasped, but he did as he was told; he couldn't think of any alternative.

Steve was standing by the rear doors, a small black gun in his hand, his bulging watery eyes watching them dispassionately. By the right headlight, Mac was huge, crop-headed and sunken-eyed, an elbow resting on the bonnet.

Both of the men were wearing shirts and jackets; their faces were expressionless. Stubble picked out the scar tissue running down Steve's neck, vanishing into his shirt collar.

– Now, said Steve. Here's what we're going to do. You, I assume, were planning to move this vehicle to somewhere discreet, yet... handy for your cottage. Am I right?

Nick was staring at the wall of the ambulance in front of him.

Paolo nodded spasmically.

– Good, said Steve, signalling to Mac to search them. Then, you'll have something for us, I think?

Mac stopped, his hands open, inches from Paolo's shoulders.

– Steve... he started.

– Mac, said Steve, a venomous edge to his voice. I pay you! Alright? *I* pay *you*... I am in charge here, and we do not come all the way out to Wales without making a profit. Okay? Now, listen to me. Alkalai?

– Yes, said Paolo weakly. We have.

– Good, said Steve, without smiling. Then, you two, get in the front. Put your hands on the dashboard. Do not move them till I tell you... Mac. In the back. Let's go.

Pete had been about to go after Belle when the smashing started. The squirrels were bounding across the attic, joist to joist, as Angus had once said they did. Except, on this occasion, something seemed to get in their way.

A cracking noise came down through the ceiling, the sound of something ripping, something else shattering; and a moment later some kind of glass receptacle dropped from the top of the stairwell and exploded halfway down it, showering droplets out into the room.

No-one moved. A squirrel crossed the last part of the attic and squeezed onto the climbing rose. Pete looked from Fay, to Angus, to Tim, who was a foot from the mouth of the stairwell – about to go up – inspecting his hands and forearms, dabbing at them suspiciously with the hem of his T-shirt.

– Wha…? Tim croaked. What the fuck?!

Pete started across the room, weaving among the chairs.

– I've no idea, said Angus. I swear to God.

The stairs were spread with a mess of tinfoil, broken glass and a transparent liquid that was trickling into a puddle on the third step. Pete arrived beside Fay, squinting at it, taking in the tinfoil, trying to alter the course of his thoughts.

– Pete… said Angus. He put an arm round Fay's waist. Pete. You don't think…?

– Has it gone on yous? he said.

– I… said Angus. It might have done. Pete, you don't think?

Pete inhaled carefully, rubbing his temples.

– Tim, he said. If I told you, that was… acid, yeah? What would you say?

Tim glanced at the smoke-browned plaster of the ceiling, then bent down, peered at the wreckage on the stairs and chuckled.

– Tim, I'm serious!

– Okay, okay, Tim sniffed at it. Like… Well, like, acid's light-sensitive, yeah? I mean, tinfoil's what people use to protect it. But, I mean, this smells of alcohol. So – I don't know

– I guess it might be, like… impure d-LSD tartrate solution or something.

– Fuck! said Pete. Fuck! Get some water!

Fay and Angus were running towards the utility room already, turning on the tap.

– I mean, it would be quite interesting, though, Tim went on. Like, as an experiment or whatever. That's how Albert Hoffman discovered what it did in the first place. You know? Getting it on his skin… I mean, it was only fifty micrograms or something – like, *millionths* of a gram – and he was completely off his face!

The ambulance lurched over the potholes in the gateway, roaring as it started up the hill. Paolo was driving, both hands shakily on the steering-wheel, the hedges seven feet tall to either side of him, blotting out everything beyond.

After the first incline the track levelled off, following the hillside as far as the farmyard. Paolo hadn't driven anything in months and he was struggling, slowing for another cluster of potholes. Nick was fretting on the seat beside him. Steve was watching them round a corner of the curtain.

– Right, he said, as a barn appeared ahead of them. This is how it's going to be. Nick. You are going to go and fetch the acid. A hundred million micrograms of it, as we agreed… Okay?

There was the dull click of metal as he screwed a silencer onto his gun. Nick nodded violently. They were passing between barns, arriving in the empty, weed-specked yard.

– Steve, said Paolo. Steve, you know we didn't set you up!

– It hardly matters, though, does it? Steve was checking round the yard, looking for signs of life. The fact is, they know who you are… When – or if – they find you, they will screw you till they get their confession. So we wouldn't be happy till

there was a very convincing reason why you'd keep your mouth
shut.

– We would, though! said Paolo.

He stopped the engine on the uphill side of the gate, still
feeling sick.

– So, said Steve. Can you see anyone else here?

– N... No, said Paolo.

– No, said Steve. Neither can I.

He pulled the trigger abruptly; the gun was quiet as a
blowpipe. The bullet passed straight through Paolo's calf and
buried itself in the floor. Paolo sucked in air as Steve clamped a
T-shirt across his face. He screamed, but the T-shirt pressed tighter
so the noise became something like the distant call of an animal.

Steve turned the barrel slowly and pointed it at Nick's
temple, pulling Paolo's head back against his shoulder.

– Nick, he enunciated. I am going to give you... eight
minutes to retrieve my property.

He removed the T-shirt and Paolo sucked in air again,
doubling forwards, blood appearing from the bottom of his flare
and running down a groove in the rubber mat.

– S... Steve, said Nick. Steve, it takes fifteen, at least! It's
right over the fields. You've got to cross a stream...

– Eight! said Steve. His face was thin and intent. His eyes
were fishlike. And if you are not back within eight minutes, I
will put a bullet through this fucker's head... Okay?

Inspector Hooey separated the last bits of egg and cress from
the crust of his ageing sandwich, eating what he could of it and
depositing the rest in its triangular packaging. He looked
around him for a bin – peering through his aviator-style
sunglasses – but nothing seemed suitable so he pushed it
discreetly down the side of his seat.

Beyond the thick, eye-like glass in front of him, the Malverns were approaching: a wall at the end of Worcestershire, green, yellow and red in the morning sunshine. The helicopter climbed to pass above them, its shadow receding as they ascended, flickering over the streets that lined the hillside, rising onto trees, quarries, walkers and concrete footpaths, closing again for a moment on the ridge before plummeting away into Herefordshire.

Hooey was in the observers' seat, a sandy-haired pilot beside him muttering occasionally into his headset. He had a map open on his lap and was checking the grid reference that they had received from the phone that morning. The computer had shown a location close beside a deciduous wood – near the edge of a field – but he was hoping further detail might reveal a barn or a cottage of some sort: anything that could be used as a hide-out.

But the new map showed no more than the old one, so Hooey refurled it and passed it back to Teather, who was working on a laptop in the seat normally occupied by a paramedic. The remaining two seats contained surly-looking men in body armour, rifles between their legs.

Hooey faced the brown-green quilt of Herefordshire nervously. He fiddled with his moustache, his eyes on the distant line of the Welsh mountains.

212

When Nick was scared, he did as he was told. It had always been the same with him. It was like his mind and his body would separate, his body moving mechanically while his thoughts panicked, repeating whatever had scared him in the first place mantra-like till he just couldn't focus at all.

He arrived outside the door, sweating and muddy, about two minutes after leaving the yard. For a moment he hesitated, trying to think of an excuse to tell the others; but all he could think of was Steve shooting Paolo – the intake of breath, the stifled screaming.

Nick pressed the latch, and pushed open the door.

Pete pulled himself up from the table immediately, his dreadlocks piled on the top of his head and the veins standing out on his forehead. Tim was rolling a joint beside the woodburner. Fay was sitting on Angus's lap at the other end. The flagstones had water all over them, and everyone but Pete had wet hair and clothes.

– You fucking bastard! said Pete, grabbing Nick by the shoulders and propelling him towards the stairwell. Look what you've done! Look!

On the stairs, the puddles were starting to evaporate. The flask was lying on the third step, part of it drooping from the edge. Nick stared at it, frozen. He managed a few noises – part defence and part incomprehension – then his body took over and he sprang into the stairwell, vaulting the acid and heading for the spare bedroom.

– Listen to me! he shouted, as he dragged the naval trunk back beneath the trapdoor, standing the stool on top of it. Listen to me! There's two men up in the ambulance, in the yard, they were waiting for us in the layby... They've shot Paolo! I'm fucking serious! They've fucking shot Paolo! He's up there with blood fucking everywhere, and if I'm not back in, like, five minutes, they're going to fucking kill him!

Nick scrambled up to the hole as quickly as he could, shoving the chipboard to one side and pushing his head through the picture frame. The roofspace was scattered with the remnants of the tent and the chromatography column. Light spread from a space in the floor above the stairwell where a section of plasterboard was hanging from a nail.

The cool-box was still where he'd left it: on a joint between joists. He pulled on the rubber gloves lying on its lid, his flick-knife

213

pressing awkwardly against his stomach as he disconnected the battery, picked it up and lowered himself back into the bedroom.

– Don't try and stop me! he shouted. Please! They might just kill us anyway, but if I don't get back – I swear to God – they'll come down here and they'll fucking kill you too! You've got to believe me – get out the fucking house!

Belle was climbing the gate on the left-hand side of the field below the yard when Nick appeared over the gate at the top of it. His head was bare, shiny in the sunlight; his feet were sliding on the muddy grass. He was running like someone was chasing him, his mouth wide open, his chin pulled back into his neck.

For a moment Belle paused, perched on the top bar. But if Nick were alone then Paolo would still be up in the ambulance, and she really didn't feel up to seeing anyone, even if it did mean fetching her cigarettes.

She jumped down into the next field, stepping carefully over the ruts and setting off diagonally up the hill, her cheeks streaked with mascara and her hands pushed deep in her pockets. She just couldn't work out why she was so upset. It wasn't as if she cared about Angus that much, and Fay – well, it was absurd. But whenever she thought of them – embarrassed, but so obviously radiant – it always seemed to make her start crying.

214   At the top of the field, Belle climbed another gate and set off left along the track. The hedges were tall, thick and browning. Between them, the clouds flowed sideways, shrinking steadily, the sky itself pale and autumnal.

She'd been walking for some minutes when she heard an engine and a Land Rover appeared around a corner in the track ahead of her, bouncing on the potholes, a red-faced grey-haired man in the driver's seat and a sheepdog peering round the canvas at the back. She pressed herself back against the hedge, lowering her eyes, shaking her head so a few strands of hair swung across her face.

– Hello, said the man, stopping beside her. You alright?

– I'm fine, said Belle quickly, her eyes still pointing downwards.

The man paused.

– You do look a bit upset, he said.

Belle pushed her hands deeper into her pockets. She waited a second, then glanced up at him, and saw only a paternal kind of concern. There wasn't a whiff of salaciousness about him.

– I… she said haltingly. It's nothing. I… I just had a bit of an argument. That's all…

– You're one of Angus's friends, are you?

– I'm his… ex-girlfriend, said Belle, and started crying again.

– Ah, said the man understandingly. Well, I'm Philip Lloyd… You'll have met my wife. Last night?

– Yeah, Belle nodded.

She wiped her eyes with her cardigan.

– Look, he said. If you want to get out of that cottage for a few minutes, come back for a cup of tea if you like… I'm going for one now anyway, and Mary'll be back in a few minutes. I'm sure she'd like to see you.

– Oh… said Belle.

– Don't worry if you don't feel like it.

– Oh… said Belle. Thankyou!   215

– Here you are, then. He leant to his left and pushed open the passenger door. Climb in round here… There's an old wing mirror down by your feet there, if you want to clean your face up a bit.

In the kitchen the mood had moved on from vengeful. The look on Nick's face had shaken Fay worse than she knew what to do about, and now there were these other two men to be accounted for: two men, a gun and Paolo with a bullet-wound. Any hope Fay had had of coming up calmly had pretty well deserted her. She wrapped her hands around her neck, desperately trying to make sense of it all.

– We've got to do something! she said, looking at Pete, then down at Angus. Like... We could go through the roof any moment now. If Nick's telling the truth and we haven't even tried to do anything, we'll... we'll be crucified! You know? We'll be fucked on! At least we should ring the police...

Something fell over upstairs and Nick's footsteps resumed on the kitchen ceiling.

– No phone, said Pete. We should just get the fuck out of here before yous lot come up.

– There's one on the main road, said Angus. By the layby.

Nick appeared abruptly at the bottom of the stairwell, stepping over the puddle, a small white cool-box in his arms and his hands in rubber gloves. His trousers were covered in mud. His face had the same, shocked, vacant expression it had had before.

– Is that...? said Tim, gawping at him. Acid?!

Nick said nothing. He set off quickly round the edge of the kitchen.

216   – Nick! said Fay.

– Don't try and stop me!

– Nick, listen! said Fay. Listen to me! Why don't... You could spike them! She tore a strip from the curtain on the table. You could dip some of this in the acid, and... wipe it on the cool-box or something!

Nick paused in the doorway. He blinked a few times, and frowned. Then he took the length of white cloth Fay was offering and hurried back towards the stairwell, dunking it several times in the puddle. He rolled it up carefully, sat it on the lid of the cool-box, and vanished back into the garden.

When he arrived at the top of the field, Nick paused again. He felt like he was about to collapse and start palpitating. Checking round the gatepost, the ambulance was still in its corner: a barn beside it and Paolo slumped in the passenger seat, his eyes half-closed and his head against the window. Nick unwrapped the length of curtain and wrung it quickly over the lid, rubbing the liquid evenly across the top, sides, and the middle of the handle. He threw the cloth into the hedge behind the water trough, swung the cool-box into the yard, then – meticulously – removed his gloves.

The gate rattled as he climbed over it.

– Alkalai...

Nick could hear Steve's voice in the back of the ambulance: tight and South London. Stopping at the driver's window – holding the cool-box by the unrubbed ends of its handle – Nick cleared his throat, waiting for instructions, looking at Paolo as his eyes flickered open.

Steve checked briefly beneath the curtain.

– Right, he said. Nick. Open the door and put it on the seat.

From somewhere to his left Nick thought he heard the sound of a diesel engine, but it was distant and he thought nothing more of it, doing as he was told then wiping his hands thoroughly on his jeans.

Mac ducked beneath the curtain, seized the cool-box with his enormous hands and removed it into the back.

– Right... he growled.

– Okay, said Steve. Now, I'm going to check this thing over, just to see exactly what we've got. Nick, you are going to get into the driver's seat, put your hands on the steering-wheel and stay exactly where you fucking are.

Across the seat, Paolo had started moaning to himself. There was a click as the lid of the cool-box opened, and suddenly, as Nick was pulling himself inside, the engine sound loudened, and a dirty green Land Rover appeared in the wing mirror beside him – a hundred yards down the track, steering round the potholes.

– Who the fuck is that?! said Mac.

Nick looked, then leant out of the sliding door and stared as it passed them, coming to a halt on the slope beside the house.

– It's… he said. It's the farmer, and… a girl.

– Okay, so why the fuck isn't this flask full?! said Steve.

The doors of the Land Rover swung open and Belle and Mr Lloyd got down into the yard, talking for a moment across the seat, gesturing towards the ambulance. Then Mr Lloyd set off towards the house – a collie wagging behind him – and, after a moment, Belle started down the hill towards them.

– Well?!

– Steve… hissed Nick. She's coming this way!

– Nick, said Steve. His voice was livid now. Where the fuck is the rest of this flask?! A third of it's not here! That's a hundred fucking grand!

– Steve, for Christ's sake! said Mac. Let's just get out of here!

– Listen, said Steve. I am not giving up a hundred grand for any fucking girl! Okay?! Get the fuck rid of her!

A moment later, Belle was at the open driver's door, pushing her hair back from her face, smiling weakly and glancing up at Nick.

– Hi, she said. Is, er… Is the back open? I need to get my cigarettes.

– No, said Nick.

Paolo had managed to pull himself upright. He was hunched to conceal his leg, his face behind his hair.

Belle looked at him curiously.

– Paolo? she said. What's going on?

– Here, why don't you have mine? said Nick, producing a packet of Lambert & Butler and proffering it. I, um… There's something wrong with the lock on the back doors.

Paolo turned slightly to look at her, his face bloodless, bruised and bearded, dark beneath the eyes.

– Paolo? Belle repeated.

– Okay… Steve's voice was quiet, icy again. His face was in shadow. The curtain flicked open and the long, silenced barrel of the gun swung out across the seat. Put your hands out…

But when he saw Belle he hesitated. She had stepped back reflexively and was staring up at the space in the curtains. Her hair was loose, shining in the sunlight. Her eyes were wide and mascaraed. Her cardigan was open, exposing a strip of stomach and cleavage. Her skin was flawless.

Steve only paused for a moment – for long enough to inhale – but Paolo threw himself on the gun unthinkingly and wrenched it downwards, pulling Steve forwards, collapsing with the effort, the gun coming loose from his fingers and discharging into the rubbish on the floor. Steve threw himself after it, but Nick had it by his feet and he kicked it out into the yard, removing the flick-knife from his waistband, releasing the blade and – in an instant – burying it in his back.

The scream this time was unhampered, guttural and incredulous. The knife jarred against his shoulderblade and caught in his sinews. Blood fanned across the grey wool of his jacket.

– Belle! Nick shouted, jumping out after the gun, chasing round the bonnet. Pick it up! Pick it up!

Across the seat, Paolo had slid open his own door and had fallen into the yard, moving dreamily. Steve was floundering, shouting, blocking off the back with his convulsions.

219

Nick wrapped his arms round Paolo's chest and began to drag him backwards up the hill towards the house, over earth and clumps of weeds. Belle had picked up the gun and was ahead of them, whimpering, pointing it randomly around her. In front of her, the house's back door was ajar. Paolo was heavy, groaning faintly. Nick was watching as Mac shoved Steve to one side and landed in the driver's seat.

The starter motor churned, stopped, churned again.

– Belle, shoot them! Nick shouted.

There was a trail of blood in the dirt from Paolo's leg. Nick felt his arms beginning to weaken. The engine came alive and the ambulance moved forward.

– Belle! Nick was screaming now. Fucking shoot them!

Belle stopped between the barn and the farmhouse, staring as the ambulance approached, its bonnet gleaming white and the specks of clouds on the windscreen. Nick's arms gave way. He went to pick Paolo back up, but looked again at the ambulance, his whole body quivering; then he turned and ran for the door as Belle – finally – began to shoot.

Her first shot hit the windscreen, turning it into a web of white lines. Her face was amazed rather than terrified, the gun held close to her chest. On the ground beside her Paolo was trying to move, his face invisible beneath his hair. Momentarily Belle glanced at him, and at the space where Nick had been, then the ambulance hit the slope and she pushed the gun desperately away from her, peering along the silencer. Her second shot glanced from the radiator. Her third flew away across the yard. But her hands were beginning to steady now, and her fourth punched another hole in the windscreen.

The ambulance was barely two seconds away when it slewed from its course, colliding with the barn to its left, bowing the corrugated-iron door. Belle was still firing – silently – her face set with determination. The walls of the barn boomed together, like the soundbox of a guitar.

It was no more than a minute later that Pete first heard the sound of rotor blades. The four of them were at the top of the field above the cottage, looking across the valley through a space between the barns. Belle had been over there, that much they were sure of. They had watched as the ambulance headed back towards the track, but who had been inside it they had really no idea.

Angus and Fay started running moments later – evenly matched – balancing their way across a tiny footbridge over a weed-choked pond and vaulting a stile at the other end.

– Tim, come on! said Pete, setting off after them, looking back.

A helicopter was floating over the quarries in the hill opposite: tiny, glass-nosed, its bodywork black with a camera poking from one side. The air around them was starting to pulse. Tim was peering at him across the stubble, grinning maniacally.

By the time Pete had climbed over the stile and arrived in the next field, Fay and Angus were almost in the one beyond it. Pete followed them along the footmarked verge between the furrows and the wood, his breath tarry, his dreadlocks bouncing against his back.

He stopped as the helicopter dropped into the field beside him, deafening, leaves rising in waves from the bare lines of earth, a door on its right swinging open and the inspector with the moustache jumping down, shouting something, struggling through the down-draught towards him.

– They're in the ambulance! Pete shouted back, guessing the question.

The inspector cupped his ear against the gale. His eyes had an eagerness about them that Pete found surprisingly endearing.

– Here! he shouted. I'll show you!

Angus and Fay stopped running when the helicopter appeared above the field behind them and they saw its insignia. They retraced the verge as far as a gateway in the wood, watching the helicopter – its rotor blades circling – then Pete and Hooey as they climbed aboard, talking excitedly.

The draught was making eddies and spirals in the air around them that – it struck Angus suddenly – seemed somehow to have been there all along, as if they'd been waiting to be realised.

– Divine wind, said Fay.

– Porcoddue, said Angus.

They watched as the helicopter took off again, leaning to the left and growing faint behind the wood. The leaves settled back to the ground. Angus and Fay sat down on the verge, putting their feet on the nearest ridge.

– I'm… tripping, said Angus, looking at her.

– Me too, she said, looking back.

It wasn't an oppressive kind of feeling, more of an acute sense of elevation. The two of them watched the sky in front of them, fascinated by it as if it were a display of the Northern Lights.

222 The sky was enormous, as was the field. Both curved away from them, following the sphericality of the earth. Angus felt a sudden, overwhelming urge to lie face down, put his arms out and hug it.

– I, um… he started, turning to Fay to explain this, but the idea shone so plainly from her face already that they could only start giggling, joining hands and inspecting each other.

Her face was pale – grinning – her hair spreading to either side of it and her eyes shining with amusement. Angus leant forward and for a while they kissed, colours evolving and unfolding in their eyelids.

– Where does the track go? said Fay, when they finished, looking through the gateway into the wood.

– The track… said Angus. He stood up, teetering. The track was rutted and grassy. It curled to the left and vanished around a corner. The track goes… anywhere!

– Well, said Fay. She sounded impressed. Then, let's go down the track!

Pete was squashed into the space between Hooey and the men with the rifles, pointing out the track to Pentwyn and its junction with the long grey line of the road. When they banked, his dreadlocks swung like a plumbline. He'd never been in a helicopter before. He had to admit it was impressive.

You could see everything from up here. The brick and wood cottage at the bottom of its field, the trees following the course of the stream, Tim in a star shape on his back in the stubble, a pair of figures carrying another into the farmhouse, what appeared to be Belle sitting smoking on the garden wall, a maroon Jaguar parked behind a mound of gravel, the river, the mountains… Everything!

It was Hooey who saw the ambulance first. He was leaning forward in his seat, his hands folded anxiously. It had stopped perhaps a hundred yards outside the turning into the track, a dent around its left-hand headlight and a line of oil behind it.

– What's going to happen to them? said Pete, bending towards Hooey's ear.

– Who? said Hooey.

– Nick, said Pete. And Paolo.

– Oh… Hooey frowned. He looked as if he hadn't given the matter much thought. I'd… urge them to co-operate, frankly. You'd be astonished what a little co-operation can do.

A figure was moving down the middle of the main road beneath him, heading vaguely towards the layby. He was hugely built, smartly dressed, and had the cool-box pinned beneath his left arm.

He was only stepping on the lines in the middle of the road, Pete realised; and as he arrived on the straight before the layby these lines became a sequence of dashes. Had he simply run he might just about have made it to his car in time, but leaping from dash to dash was slower progress. The dashes were narrow and several feet apart, with cat's-eyes to encounter in between them. Pete could imagine what it would be like down there. The terror of the black and the brilliance of the white – he'd been in enough similar conditions. You had only to see the distinction once and that was it: the white spelt safety, familiarity, comfort, while the black became the unknown, the great dark emptiness, where anything at all might happen.

z: ...shining.

I was unsure whether my eyes were closed or open. I was unsure even whether I had eyes at all. I may have been facing up or down. I may have been cold, or hot, or distinct from all of these things.

It did, however, seem that I possessed a memory of pain in my left leg, another in my pelvis; an idea that my eardrums had been damaged in some way, by the sound of my own voice, by the explosion that had driven me up and into the canopy.

It was dark. That much I could be sure about. It was dark and in some way I was floating. I had not, of course, known how events would unfold once the mission was over, but I continued to expect the handmaidens of the Kami to materialise at any moment, to take me in their arms and carry me towards the light of Yasukuni. Yet as the seconds – the hours or years – elapsed, I became aware that my thoughts were growing vaguer again, fiery in some way. Panic was pressing itself upon me. I had an overwhelming sensation of confinement and powerlessness.

Perhaps, it occurred to me, I was capable of moving myself. Perhaps for a mere student – a humble conscript – it was an arrogance to expect help from those beautiful maidens, whose images I knew so well from my upbringing. The darkness seemed not only to be enveloping me, but to be infusing my very core.

The light appeared suddenly, faint through the flexing blackness. In some moments it was a circle, in others fragmented. I willed myself towards it, scarcely conscious when I broke the ocean surface. My head spun in the waves, craning backwards to cough down air. Above me the moon was huge – white, full – clear even to my salt-damaged eyes.

It was just as I was slipping back into blackness that I heard a sound nearby. A foreign shout of some kind. Fighting to remain afloat, I found myself suddenly in a light of such brilliance that it might have been the sun. I could see only whiteness, feel only the coarse hands that took me by the neck, tugging me backwards into a dinghy and throwing me to the floor where my left leg crumpled beneath me.

The blindness dissolved slowly into a line of barking faces, the reek of alcohol, the dark lines of the gunwales. An ornately dressed man was pushing his way towards me, stepping over the thwarts, the crowd parting in front of him. He stopped, astride – his face contorted with anger – but even as I was, sodden and shivering, I might have been new-born.

He held no fear for me of any kind.